MW00801099

POVERTY UNPACKED

Knowing EPRDF From Its Fruits

DANIEL L. ASFAW

PublishAmerica
Baltimore

Hardcover 978-1-4512-2028-5
Softcover 978-1-4512-2066-7
PUBLISHED BY PUBLISHAMERICA, LLLP
www.publishamerica.com
Baltimore

Printed in the United States of America

Political Inspired
Collection of Short Stories

This book is dedicated to my beloved mother the late Bizunesh Bekel Cheregne and my younger sister the late Emebet Legesse Asfaw. They were my biggest universities where I could get the most wisdom that life could give. Leave alone their striking respective life styles; the incidents of their individual passing away were lessons that I could have never grasped within a century.

ACKNOWLEDGEMENT

All of us embarked on an already instigated vim and vigor. One cannot possibly quote some one that has started the knowledge in this universe. All of us had a pile of it to build ourselves on, except He who began the beginning on His own. King Solomon, whom we claim as his wisdom is second to none, has said it well in his *Book of Proverbs* that all knowledge starts from the fear of the lord. For him God, who said"*I am that I am'*, is the alpha and the omega of all the knowledge in all ages. Fair enough to pronounce that *He is that He is* yesterday, today and forever more.

This piece of work has much to do with the divine assistance I had from God above. It is He who very splendidly gave me the inspiration, the motivation and even the strength to do it. Otherwise, writing such politically inspired fictional story would mean a kind of *"put me to the death"* act. This is so because the book, through short fictional stories, unpacks the inside-out with regard to current Ethiopia and its people. What is the truth of life in that country where the rules and governance of EPRDF is turning into creed? It is evident that if any politics is not well handled it turns out to be a religion and its leader will start to receive worship, in fact, without having any divinity. Hitler was a good example since he was standing in the shoes of God for many, and Nazism as scriptures and doctrines while his party the church of his believers.

How does that people live life in Ethiopia? Aren't they made worship EPRDF, in fact, forcefully? Do they have a freedom to be a non-EPRDF citizen and still maintain to get what that country has for its residents? I mean the answer is clear, if one is not saved from the spirit of opposition by the might of the gospel of 'Zenawi' there is no hope for better life in Ethiopia, in fact, in the wake EPRDF. Yes, baptism is required, getting impressed in the stream of their though and believe. These guys are their own creators; they need people not only to follow them, but also to bow before their majesty. They are the law themselves. They jail and can kill, if they so.

I always bear in mind the inexplicable death incident of his Excellency Balu Girma, the father of Modern literature in Ethiopia and the author of those superbly written books as *"Keadmas Bashager", "Derasiw", "Yekey Kokob Tiry"* and many more, who vanished right after writing his last book entitled *"Oromay"* for a sheer reason that he wrote about the reality of the big bosses in the Dregs' regime. These great creams of the crop where untouchable, somehow he dared to lay a hand on them and in no time he hazed like a vapor to the unknown. Till date no one can point out where the hell he has gone to.

In Ethiopia writing the truth was as demanding as it is today. It has claimed many authors their own precious lives. Though, history has hidden the truth, I guess, many who were writing against the system of their own times have been murdered by the juntas of their days. Still, were/are many who are killed and/or put to the jail lawlessly for writing the truth of the society they live in.

That could be one of the possible reasons, I guess, for most of our forefather writers who wrote a lot of lies to us about our kings and their loved ones to write such stories of angles for human beings. They weren't ashamed to put their pens to paper to write about some of our kings as if they were celestial beings exquisitely appointed by God and were from the family tree of Jesus Christ.

They wrote what they were told to write. If they refused to do that the other option was plain clear. It was either death or jail. Some have actually drunk the cup of their sorrowful but historic death for writing the truth of their time.

Those days of the so-called 'monarchies and/or Dergs' have gone; nevertheless situations are slow to change. Nowadays, instead of "kings" we have the "Prime Minister" who wants us to note down his mind, never allowing us to think and act according to our own informed impulse. He and the people around his table of 'headship', not to say leadership, deem as if they are the master mind. They believe they are in actual fact they are the designer cosmos. For them man is just a biological incident, nothing better than that, just as simple as that. If they kill him, it is nothing different than killing a protozoario. They never care about it, though, they pretend they do.

Nevertheless, they never think of themselves that same way. They feel they are the super natural. They act as if they are the law. In short, they have many untouchables as their historical predecessors who passed in that same line of 'headship' in Ethiopia. Who knows, they may even think that they are reigning over the crown of the Lord. They may believe that they are the powers and makers of the world. They can jail, torture and even kill, if somebody is not in accordance with their thinking. They are free to do their wishes, since they are the law, themselves.

Who can sneer at these giants unless by super natural push? I am not saying I have dared enough, this is just a begging; and this much beginning was possible by the mighty of He who set the thing in motion deep in my heart. Hence, if at all I am thankful to anyone, He is the one that takes all my praises and thanks without limit. In short I am grateful to my Lord for motivation and encouragement within me, the good words in the stories, and the competence in the area.

I am also thankful to my wife and children who have helped me thus far in passing this great assertion of writing this hardback of short stories that artistically unveils the reality with regard to the poverty of Ethiopia to the whole world. My God-given wife, Sara G. Kinfe, is a great woman that always has lesson to educate me in all walks of our life together. I have learned a lot from her and with her more than I did in my school days.

My children are also my good schools where I read from the human mind un-limitlessly deep and wide. They have practically educated me the hard way my parents have gone through to grow me to this height. They have also shown me the quintessence of true love. I truly love them for reasons that I can't tell. And by so doing I have learnt so much about the love of my divine father in the heavens.

These children have a lot to be comprehended if one has the open-mindedness to learn and find out the truth all around us. Hence, I should be thankful to my God-given wife and the three children I am entrusted to grow for the purpose they are created to.

My younger brother and his wife whom I am not comfortable to mention their name here have also given me a kind of the necessary vigor and vitality to go about writing this book. In particular, the bravery I used to get from my brother whom I am very much proud of as he is a hard working Ethiopian who managed to write and stage three long lived full scale plays and one wide-reaching and most renowned dramatic movie, counts beyond words to articulate.

He was in point of fact the strongest backup I had whenever I was staked in the process of writing this book. May I wish many happy and good returns to him in this juncture of acknowledging the inputs of those very great people without whose contributions i this book would have remained to be a dream?

I would also like to thank my uncle-cum-brother Dr. Yilma Bekele who foresaw my destiny while I started the journey and called me Doctor. I was just a little kid almost nobody in the eyes of many by the time he used to call me "Doctor". He has always been my encouragement and support whenever I get tired of my abettors. His counsel, good words and guidance all across my life till date is remarkably unforgettable. I have learned so much so to speak from him. My respect and affection from him is so august.

Of all, my greatest indebtedness goes to my readers who will read this book and find out what is going on in Ethiopia, the first genital nation to believe in Jesus Christ and accept Christianity from all other countries in the world expect for Israel. How are Ethiopians today? How do they manage life? What a hell is keeping them in the strongholds of poverty thus long? Hope this book gives us a little about the realty on the ground and even it may motivate us for due action in a proper way. That is the goal of this book—getting as many eyes as possible to read and understand the Ethiopia of today. Hence, the lion's share of my gratitude goes to those who will read the book and understand the gist in it.

PREFACE

Is Ethiopia actually poor? This is a serious question a thousand years of research may not address very well. Since Ethiopia is a country of ancient civilization, may be next to Greek and Egypt with a history of 3000 years, it would be hasty to generalize Ethiopia as a poor country on the basis of some visible indicators. The rock hewn churches here and there in the country, the castles of long time kings, the paintings and the work of arts in the monasteries, the obelisks and other many more realities on the ground give patent evidence that Ethiopia was in fact a great country with a glorious past.

The Holy Bible in more than 50 location of its over its 66 books exhibits and make known the fact that Ethiopia is a country of special purpose in the eyes of God. That is the reason; I guess, that it is mentioned as many times as second to Israel, the prime country of God, in the whole Bible. It obviously illustrate us the fact that Ethiopia is the first gentile nation receiving Jesus Christ as seen in the book of Acts 8:26-28 which talks about that unique Ethiopian eunuch who was preached by Philip.

Where has that glory gone to today? What is special in our time? What's up man? What a hell has taken away that wonderful time in the country? Could it be the states and their systems that have passed along the way leading the nation to this endless depression? It is because the society has lost its work ethics entirely and has come poles apart with the people in the past? I really wonder!!!

After all what is poverty, indeed? Is it a paucity of money or lack of good relationships and wherefrom, of course, lack of access to basic needs of life? I think, everything starts with understanding what poverty signifies. For me poverty is all about relationship; relationship with God the Most High, relationship with self the most honored and loved being ever, relationship with others our own most beloved brothers, and finally relationship with the milieu all around us the most essential creation ever made by the creator. Paucity of possession and wealth alone can't signify poverty.

All the said relations have to be well maintained in order for someone to be leveled poor or reach. Our issues today are issues of relationship. Man is fighting first of all with himself, everywhere. Most of us are never honest to our own inner most man and as a result we could never be candid to others and ended up in a perpetual kind of conflict, everyday in hostility with our inside.

As if trying to put fire in the fuel, EPRDF has damaged the already broken relationship that people have with themselves across the nation. That beautiful country of over 80 nations and nationalities has turned to be a battle field of neighborhoods. It is just a kind of time bomb that EPRDF is burring under the soil of the entire nation when it comes into relationship issues. The lack of fairness, justice and democracy allover in the country is heating the shell to fire sometimes in the near future.

This collection of short stories is a reflection of some of the symptoms of this shocking relationship between the government and its people in Ethiopia. It tries the hardest to unpack how this relationship is broken across the county. It exhibits some of the *'hidden evils'* today that has kept our people from trying hard to break the shell of poverty and become somebody. To this end, it brings close to 25 shorts stories all based on the true stories as observed by the author in Ethiopia and may be elsewhere. These stories may highlight on not only the level of poverty in the said nation by large but also on what makes humankind poor as well.

Hence, those concerned need to open their eyes together with their hearts and see the lives of their people and choose what actions they should take to curve the situation. The path on poverty has no end unless we bend it somewhere. It is easy to do it. It needs to build the right type of relationship governed by justices and fairness among people that we are responsible for.

If we put our hands on our mouth and see while people are abusing nations we are poor ourselves. These people will tend to affect others and eventually will be dangers for the whole of humanity by large. We have to stop them from being too evil and show them the right thing to do. Literature, as reflection of life, is one way to educate them about what is going around. If they could learn and tempted to take action this is the time. It will really be too costly to curve things after the thing has well taken off. That is what this book is for. It is a warning bell to the concerned stakeholders in the country and around the world calling for help to rescue Ethiopia from the jaws of death created as a result of bad ascendancy by EPRDF. It is true EPRDF will go, but the people will remain behind.

The book advices humanity not to be candy coated even as politicians and leaders of a nation. Most of us are sweet on the cover and aching deep down, aren't we? Can't we at least the same sweet to the end, if we can't go well? This book urges us to be like clean water in a clean glass, so that what one may see outside is what is actually inside. The time demands our honesty to whatever relationship we have with our God, ourselves, others and the environment. We have to be good in whatever we think and whatever we do in this petite planet if we are so concerned about somebody better than us.

EPRDF is just one example of relations polluters. There could be more of the same elsewhere in the world. EPRDF might have committed the sin while dividing between people on the basis of who they are. That is as perilous as it broke up many families as seen across the nation. The seed of hatred sawn by the sitting government has not yet started to be harvested. The worst is yet to come, I guess. Many blood shades and civil wars may not make the end of the reaping season yet to come. Relationship has been seriously damaged among different ethnic groups, between themselves, within self and across.

It is the purpose of this book to cry the tears of the victims of this broke up relationship in Ethiopia as just one incident that could happen anywhere in the world. What could EPRDF learn from this book? How about the rest of the world? Ignorance and resistance couldn't make the answer. We have to try our level best to wave the weeds we planted in the soft soils of the nation. It is not too late to do it, if need be.

Eventually, I would like to underscore the fact that all the characters, be it male or female, that I have used in the short stories published in this book are fictional and do not represent anyone from anywhere in this world. The stories are, therefore, the stories of these characters that I myself have created to live and die in the imagination world I have fashioned only for them. Nonetheless, the purpose of their creation is to depict the reality in Ethiopia today. In fact, I have inculcated some two short stories that portray the life situations in some other places for diversity sake. After all, I always ponder the fact that literature has no other significant work than reflecting the reality of the real world.

WOMAN ON THE CROSS

"He was like 15 years of age when I was banned from going to my school by the agents of EPRDF. I was like a seven years kid by then. I remember my mother divorcing her beloved husband for a mere reason that he was from a different ethnic background than what she was from. She used to pester him like a devil may torment his guys in the hell." She was, then, immediately taken by a kind of emotion bubbling out on her face. She stopped narrating the story and started struggling with her feeling, at times trying to clear the tear drops running her beautiful old looking g features.

After a while she got back into the truck, "I don't know what a hell happened between them. They weren't like that until EPRDF took power from the gun fighting and released its ethnic based politics into the atmosphere. They were so loving and caring couples I even had observed. They used to love each other like young bloods. What happened after EPRDF?" She asked herself.

The lady seems to have a lot of questions about her family than it was possible to answer. These questions about her family have changed her appearance entirely. She looks like a 75 years old woman while still 35. The lines on her face exhibit the life path she has been trough. Too much bended by saddle on her shoulder, she is completely restless and without peace. Her hair was totally gray. Her eyes are almost melting into their respective hallways. All the time they appear to be crimson as if socked in an ocean of blood. They have never been spared from tearing day in and day out.

After quite a struggle with his inside, the officer asked her how old she was.

"35" she replied.

He couldn't believe his ear, "35!" he replied with exclamation.

"Oh my goodness," He shouted deep inside. She was not able to listen to his howl. At one end he even was not sure if she was not telling him the truth. She read his mind form his facial expression and said, "Don't forget Officer that I made an auth to tell you the truth and only the truth."

He felt as if she overheard him while talking to his heart. He couldn't imagine to grasp the picture of a young lade in the skin of a 75 years old woman.

"My gash, what happened?"

"I have no idea officer. Do I look old?" She asked.

"Yes, you look totally a different woman."

"I have been locked in a dark room since 1999. I have never seen light. I am almost both blind and deaf. The only time I used to be in my won world is when sleeps was able to take me away by the mighty of its power. In fact, I used to space out a lot, trying to lose connection to this shanty world." She went away in thought as if trying to show me what she meant.

Unexpectedly, she came back to her sense and said "Sorry, You know what, at times the images of the bodies of my father and my brother could never leave me alone. It used to walk me in and out of the prison. Ones I started walking hand in glove with this thought, I used to away from self for 5 to 8 hours consecutively."

As she was narrating her story the pictures of those bodies that were street murdered came back again and filed her memory. All of a sudden, she plunged into tears. None-stoppingly she cried and wept for more than half an hour. The officer couldn't help himself. He was also sternly touched by her situation. He has never met a person relentlessly packed down by the strong holds of disastrous tyranny as she was. He tried to calm her down but he couldn't make it happen. Instead, he ended up howling himself with her.

"I was the last child of my loving and caring parents. I had five siblings of whom three of them were killed, one is reaped repeatedly, and every one of them are tortured and tormented by the ruling party."

"Sorry to interrupt you, could you please tell me why were you subject for these entire ordeals?"

"It is one and one. I believe three words can make the answer, it was just for who we are, Just our ethic background. We were classified by the party as an enemy of the rest of the nations and nationalities constituting that poor nation. You get me? In fact we also have some difference in our political views with the ruling party." She kept quiet for a while struggling with her emotion. Her eyes easily get filled with tears.

Out of the blue, she came back to her sense and continued to say "This bull government slaughters its people like a sheep just for who they are and what they think. Believe me, as a person me and my mother have never thought of our background. The only think we were concerned about was our love. She used to love me. My love for her was even more. But what to do, EPRDF came and lectured us abhorrence. They are prophets of hatred. They always preach from the gospel of devil. As a matter of fact we had a magnificent love together as couples until such time that EPRDF came to power with its poisoning ethnic politics which fall us apart."

A voice crossed her mind. It was her father who was one of the guys who were recently to be murdered on the street. She has seen his body lying with her own brothers on the street of Addis Ababa. They all were shot on either on the head or on the heart being hit with quite a number of bullets. Specially, her father was severely mutilated. It looks he was taken to be murdered on street instantly after fresh torture. His left leg was broken. His clean blood was gushing out covering on the face of the street.

The great flock of dogs which were licking the blood was not able to clean the surface at all. That image came back again and erected deep in her heart. She busted into tears again. The whole of her body was crying. She was immersed into tears. She rather became a kind of an iced tear in the human flash. Yet the voice was still speaking, vocalizing loud but very calmly.

"They broke our love, they aborted our relation, and they killed our closeness. In short, they dismantled us all. Finally, they perished us all, as one nation. That is it!" the voice was full of anger. I could sense an inflexible tone of alarm coming out from it. It was like a call that says "what are you waiting for, guys?"

"Yes it is!"
"Oh my goodness, how come it heard my whisper?" I asked myself. "It is like you become a spirit being when you get out of this sheet?" I pondered.

The lady is still in her deep dirge. The tone of the ghost couldn't give her a break. The voices of all the other ghosts are behind it. They all shouted "death to Zenawi and his regime!" The good thing is that they did not have the gun in their hands; otherwise they would have gone and killed him in person.

"Since then we hated each other and lost our sense of being together as a married couple. Simply we came to an end. My wife turned to be a bitter and painful women on me. I also lost my test of marriage and finally left her for good to become a homeless. That is just one family; the whole country is like that. That is what my country got from EPRDF. I tell you the whole haven knows, this party is responsible to the destruction of my people, bit by bit and one by one."

"At present, I live in here in this solitary confinement facing torment and torture, being deprived to be visited even by my loved ones, including my only child. I have no idea about my future home. My morrows are in the hands of the Almighty. Even if I have no knowledge about the days ahead, I know He who runs them in order. " She interrupted.
The officer was panic with this strange incident. He couldn't make a point from her interview. He felt as if he has partially lost sense.

She didn't care much about him and continued to give him a brief account of her life. "As a matter of fact I was not able to complete my grade level studies due the pressure I suntanned in my life. I only went as far as grade 10 in Black Lion Comprehensive High School in 1986 and dropped out school after completing grade 10 due to the death of my father and brothers."

She kept calm for a while. It looks she had a lot of staffs crossing her mind whenever she thinks of her school life. The chances she missed, the days she lost, the opportunities which went out her hands, what not! She reflects all about them. Actually, it is not reflection; she rather sank deep into her old days. Her memories eat her up.

Ultimately, she came back to her interview yet again. "I don't care if I am not schooled. Life is my biggest university and experience is my best teacher. I have learned al lot from my ups and downs. But what is education about? Isn't it a tool that helps the elite to run his own selfish motive? It is!"

I entrapped her in the middle of her thought. I didn't like her spacing out. Right away, I jumped into my query. "Who killed your father?" Before I finish making the question that voice came back again and answered it all. "EPRDF! That is it!" This time I was able to hear it myself as well. Not only hearing, I was able to see it nodding in assertion too.

The answer was short but clear-cut. But in no time the voice continued speaking out. "We all were murdered in the street where we used to live after we were pushed out of our home."

"What were you doing on the street? Now I started conversing with the phantom. It feels you became an angle or devil, himself. I had a pleasure to get the information but with a lot of fears. Nothing is more dreadful than the unknown.

"We used to fight EPRDF by being homeless. Since that was the only fruit they make out of their ethnic based politics. They made us a citizen of no country in our own nation. You know how many of us are driven out of home due to this politics?"

I was excited to hear the statistics. This was so because, I heard one of the top officials boldly saying that they never do any harm to their people. 'Do officials lie?' I asked myself. All of a sudden I received an answer whispering to me ear "They do, their truths are but repeated lies."

She took a while before releasing her tone of voice. In the mean time I was talking to myself. Somehow she came in to tell me the statistics. The answer was a kind of funny.

"Nobody knows the number. We are just a lot! My family is just an example. Millions are out there. Coming to the crux of the matter, as a homeless out here I used to organize the jobless youngsters in Addis Ababa to conduct a rally, raise money, and perform peaceful demonstration being hand in glove with my leading political organization, CUD (Collation for Unity and Democracy)."

"Yes that was the party I wanted to live and die for. But where is that party today?"

She just came in and asked. I nodded no. She was like half normal. I wasn't able to follow her up. She flew away a lot sometimes leaving the officer all alone in the interview room. In the mean time a voice uses her being to speak out for the killed. I wasn't sure whom I was talking with.

"Yes, that is my question. In fact everybody asks that same question. Everybody grapples with it. They breathe it like oxygen, these days. You know why, we have paid all the cost of troubles that it took the party to be successful in the national election, in fact up to death. They did, had it not been EPRDF desire to continue in power by the mighty of gun. Everybody, regardless all across the nation, voted for victory. It was the symbol of conquest for us. We had all our dreams in them, as a matter of fact."

She again was taken by deep thought. The officer himself was like board of hearing and narrating her situation. Actually, he is a good observant, but not always. He couldn't read her inside as she is. The volcanic pressure running through her blood canals, the strength the melted feelings that hear heart was trying to pump out, the pains and anguish that her beats were all about what not. He was not able to see them in bare. That was why I was trying to help portraying what was deep in this woman of broken and heart and bended hope.

Betty is one of the great women of the day that only a centre can give. She is a kind of in and out, back and forth but stubborn woman who choose to live eternity in prison than to live a life of opulence outside without freedom. The latte choice was what her spouse decided to go for. Actually he went for it, he sued his wife on the basis of false allegation, got appreciated by the fathers of sham and finally as a reward, he became a minster after putting her to perpetual jail.

"The whole thing was a miscarriage. But where are we now? How could we end up like this? Where is CUD officer? "She asked herself. She asked him as well. She asked all concerned? The officer was confused as everybody was. He was not able to understand her, neither the whole world was.

CORRUPTED BEING

"I have seen the power of death in my naked eye." said Suzy Mark. Usually many call her as "Suzy the old". Not because she is that old. She is catching her 21 but has already graduated from her own University in 'torture-logy'. "I am the third child in my family with two brothers older than me."

She was in fact energetic with a bouncing smile while speaking to her employer at the interview. After her laconic preface, her employer wanted her to tell him whether she is happy or not about the type of the job that she is going be offered.

"Are you happy to work with us here?' The employer asked her with a lucid and tender voice. It looks as if he has other third motives behind the screen.

"Sure, why not?" Suzy replied with incoherent mind. She was never sure of what the future holds for her. She knew that he has no idea what type of woman she was. She was like a bit perplexed deep inside. She felt it would be proper if she let him know inside out before even offering her the job. She was pondering how to start telling him about her.

After a long breath, Suzy came out of her dejection and said "How about telling me your life testimony? I mean a brief account of your life?"

"Sure, I want the whole world to listen to my testimony so that they may see the good things that Jesus has done in my life. I want the whole world to learn from my story and become sympathetic to humanity all around men."

He was very excited to listen to her testimony. "I once went to a nearby clinic for a medical checkup as I was constantly suffering from a chest pain. During this cheek up, the doctor understood the fact that I was very week. As days went by, he learned much about me from the symptoms I manifested and from the questions he was asking."

Both of them took some breathing. "Immediately he referred me to one of the government hospitals for further health management where we have the only cardiac clink in the nation. There I was told that I have to go for cordial surgery to get well off from my heart trouble. I came to know that the matter is so serious with me. However, I could do nothing, and neither do my family. We did not have what it would take to make me health."

Now the employer has forgotten his business and was taken long by her affectionate words. She was so sluggish, so sniveling and broken. He was like gazing on her chest as if trying to get into her heart and solve some of her health issues.

"Okay" He just wanted her to continue.

"As I was not even able to go to school, I got to be worried so much that I have no other future but death." She was a kind of carless at the start. Now situations are a bit changed. She continued to be full of tear. Her heart was pumping too much. Yet, she continued telling him her story. "I used to dream my grave at every fraction of my life. He kept on crying and my family used to morn with me." All of a sudden she plunged into an ocean of tears.

The employer tried to console her so that to get her back to the discussion. However, she was so emotional that she took some time to get dried off. The moment she got out her emotion, he asked her "Why is this much tearing on an already gone story?

"It is a tear of thanks giving not distress. You see, death was on its way to my home. Poverty was about to kill me while I was young. You know what I mean?" She paused for a while and asked him a question to help her make sure that he is listening to what she is talking about.
"Sure" he nodded.

"Well had I been in the country like USA, my cardiac problem wouldn't be a reason for death; even for those children who are from a well to do families but living in the developing countries like mine, this problem can't be considered a dying case. This is so because they can afford the cost for the cure. Don't you think so?" She paused a question. He didn't try to answer. He was just gazing at her amazing face.

After a while, she just came in and broke the silence. "I could not have enough money and as a result, the only choice I

had, as I told you, is to gulp the cup of death and in fact expire."
She again kept silent. The picture of the PM came into her
mind. His long forehead is now totally covered by sharpened
horns. She tried to count the number of the horns, but she
couldn't make it. They were as much as the number of his hairs
at the back of his head. However, as she stayed gazing at them,
they turned into 88; each one has one ethnic group pierced by it.
The fire that was coming out of his eyes had a picture of his own
wife, as if she was the one putting the whole nation in to blaze.
His bright face is totally diffused. "There is no hope." Her deep
inside whispered to her.

As the silence went too long, he asked her another question
in away to get her back to the story she was narrating, "How
could you managed to get the treatment?"

"Well to make the long story short, a non-for-profit
organization that works with children having cardiac problem
facilitated my treatment in Netherlands where I stayed for three
months and got back with full health. Isn't that a great thing for
a poor child like me? It is."

"It is indeed splendid." he replied and continued to forward
his third question "Then what?"
"I cannot forget those people, what so ever. They have set
wonderful models to my life. I love them very much, and I
would love to be like them. Coming to my secular study, as you
well know I have completed my first degree from Addis Ababa
University in Journalism."

"Can I forward my last question to you?" She gave him a
positive smile allowing him to go for the question.

"What do you like to be in the future?"

"I would like to be whatever God wants me to be. God willing I wish if I can have the opportunity to serve your organization."

"Well that is the simplest thing I can do for you. As you know I am the human resource manager. It is up to me to hire and/or fire."

She just couldn't sense the path he wanted to walk her through. He came a bit closer to her. His eyes look very emotional. His face is turning reddish. It looks his heart has stopped its other activities and started to pump his body with feel affection for her. She looked into his eyes. They saw each other in fears.

"I am moved by your story. I could see that you are a kind of woman that needs a person like me. I know you badly need my support." As he came closer to her she started to get away from him.

"What do you mean sir?"

"What do I mean?"

"Can't you read my eyes?'

"I am worried sir."

"Don't worry you will relax soon. By the way you didn't tell me about your marital life. Are you married?"

"No, I am not."

"That sounds good."

"What for?"

"Well if you want to be employed her ..." She took the words from his mouth and said "I have to lay for you?" She shouted.

"No, you shouldn't" He wanted to cool her down.

What is going on sir?"

"Since the day, you came to my office; your aroma couldn't go from my sense."

"What does that mean?"

He just couldn't tell his heart. He is like a serpent in the grass. One can't see him moving. But he always bites. That is how EPRDF moves. Nearly, all the female staff in the office has gone that way. He is married and yet he likes dating other ladies. He is never honest to his wife. He is never happy with her too. His wife knows that very well. Nevertheless, she has already two children from him. On the top of that she is a house wife. She has nowhere to go. Even if she does they can't do any good to her. They know the fact that he is one of the bulls of EPRDF. Once she has been to a lawyer for counsel.

"Well I don't have caught him red handed."

"If you don't have sound and enough evidence, written and/ or verbal, you can't win him."

"How about the ladies he has dated?"

"Well, none of them will publicly say that he has dated them."

"What if they say so?"

"Well they have to substantiate it by evidence."

From that day on wards she lives with him as a stove ash lives with fire. She is never happy with him, but has kept everything in dark. She doesn't want her children or any other third person knows the matter. However, whenever she tries to advice him not to do such immoral he gets up and leave the house up until she goes wherever she is and gets him back home apologizing for the past.

"Well what does this mean?" he came very close to her. He is totally lost. He has no control on his emotion. He looks very hot and need to have somebody to exclaim his emotion. He can't carry it long. He can never stay with it even for a fraction of second.

"I have to trash it women."
"What!"
"I have to garbage my trash."
"So what?"
"You haven't realized yet, you are the right dumpster."

Now she understood what he meant. She is so worried. She tried to leap out. She has nowhere to go. The office is locked. Soon, he looked at his watch and jumped over her and plastered his lips on hers. She jostled a lot and shouted long. Nobody was there to respond to her call for help. It was 40 minutes after office hour.

After three month she realized the fact that she was heavy with child in her womb. Pregnant from an agent of EPRDF, she sat on her own leg and cried a lot. In her tears she saw how they compel many others to make them their members this way.

BORN EXPIRED

The 23rd of September 2007 has brought an abnormal Thursday night to Repy, a miniature village, in close proximity to Woliso, south west of Addis Ababa, the capital of Africa. That night, everything was dull and hushed. The green pastures, the narrow alleyway, the small huts, the night dogs, and even the hyenas are all immersed yawningly deep into the unruffled tranquil. In short, all have surrendered to the authority of the darkness. The meadows, the clay soils, even those small huts are all covered with the dooms of the dimness. It is not easy even to trace the where about of those big trees which the community worships as its own gods.

They are now bowing for the might of the obscurity, themselves. Their might have gone to the mysterious. What is clear about them is that they are all buried in the ocean of the diffused dark. They struggle to go for a dip and still they can't move their wings of trounce an inch. They couldn't salt away the inhabitants from the strongholds of poverty. All are snowed under. "Where have my friends gone today?" said Jonathan, with a voice full of terror and horror.

His over worn old shoes has been put on for three months now. Everything he does, every cloth he wears, every word he speaks, and every drink he takes prove the fact that he is getting crazy after his ejection from the university which was followed by the loss of his beloved wife who was kidnapped days before his discharge. He doesn't know what a hell she is taken by. He tried hard and bold to figure out but couldn't manage to find her out on this planet earth.

At last, he left Addis for good a year ago to his birth place Repy, a small but productive land with people who have no access to potable water, electricity and even health stations and who can't get enough to eat even two times a day in years of abundance in the nation. They are dramatically very meager people but living on a very fertile land of opulence.

The unexpected casualty of his spouse years back has contributed for his 'wide of the mark' personality that never demonstrates who the man is. However, it is his dissatisfaction with the government that has hardened and worsened his situation. Whenever he speaks about them, he loved to say, "These are people of pretense and fabrication. They never tell the truth. They even never hear to the substance. They are enemies of legitimacy. For them we are the byproducts of their factory.

The May 7, 2005 election is a good prove to this, they were beaten everywhere. However, some how they continued to be in power again. They got to power back again by the might of gun without war, since no one was shouting against them as they were killing a lot of the voters. Given this ad other instance in the country, EPRDF will never come down until it disband by itself perhaps by nature factors or after the establishment of the middle class society some years ahead; they will never give up governing the nation."

As he walked in the darkness, he tried to look at the sky. Nothing was on the firmament. The petite moon itself has strangely concealed her from the face of the heavens. There is no glow above as there in none down. "Where have they gone? Is the heaven the reflection of the earth? Where can we cry? Who can listen to us? How many years should we be kept in the world of obscurity?" he asked himself without uttering a word.

A bit latter he stared at his wristwatch. It is 2:00 after the midnight.

"Sunday is going away."

"It is good let it go."

"The question is will you get a better Monday?"

"I don't know, how can I tell that ... but history tells us that there will come no good day."

"No, no... the trees may remain on their station, worshiped and reverenced; who knows who can deracinate them? They are deep rooted on the ground by their mighty." He laughed and then cried, smoking now and then and sipping the smock deep inside, like a silly man and concluded his dialogue with the most inner man jailed in him.

He is over drunk as accustomed. A book at his pocket hand and a cigarette at his lips are common with him. He walks with them everywhere he goes. He lives in the book like a bookworm; he smokes like kitchen; he drinks day in and day out like a fish does and drinks within a gap of a split second. As he looked straight into the huts, he hardly saw somebody at the get. "It must be Eliza." He laughed and felt contented deep inside. "I would have been a dinner for a hyena... am I not already?" He asked himself and continued his way to Eliza.

Eliza Lema, a mother of two and a wife of none, is the only one in the village that has opened her entrance to the emperor of the dim. She is a stunning young lady who has gone over eighty years of age only in her twentieth. She looks desperate and frantic in her nightwear which she uses during the day as well. Her brown face is utterly murky now.

The lines on her forehead illustrate the long journey of trail that she has covered in the world of lack. Her big eyes have started melting inside. "I have stayed thus far feeding on my body, oh lord now I want you to take my soul or give me enough to it." She begged the majesty of the darkness, looking at the sinister being in badly lit.

It is her third day without rations. There is nothing edible in the domicile, nothing except for the clay water which she fetches from the river. They eat the soil in water in the form of potage. That is all she has in the house. Her two daughters look like a body ready for burial stretched on the ground. There is no bed in the house apart from the little one that Eliza uses for commercializing her body.

Somehow Professor Jonathan reached at her gate with his book at hand and his cigarettes serving him as a torch, for quite a long time she couldn't recognize him at all. She was totally taken up by her deep thought. She was packed up by her own agony.

"Good evening!" she gave him no response. "I said good evening!" no answer again. As she couldn't respond he pulled her down towards him. "What is new today, life is in its usual orbit my sweetheart." As he is trying to embrace her and give her a kiss she was trying to get out his arms and avoid him.

"Don't touch me. I don't want to be with you tonight." She scouted at him.

"What is wrong with me my sweet?"

"I have told you I don't want to be with you. Go and look for you woman. I need somebody that can give me money while I give him myself."

"I will get you tomorrow whatever amount you wish to have."

"Forget it. That is your routine word. You have never been as good as your words."

"Why are you hot today, don't you truly know how I love you form deep down my heart?"

"I said forget it. What can love do without life?" instantly she was taken up by her bottomless thought. It looks she has a dialogue with a kind of voice coming from above.

"As you well know I have two daughters Kedija and Fatuma both are below five years of age. I have already lost my husband. He has died of AIDS three years back. He left us for good leaving us only with the virus." It looked as if she thinks all men have dead.

"What do you mean by saying that?"

"What do I mean?" she took the question deep into her mind and after a while she started to answer it.

"Well for me my husband is the only hope I had in this world. You know I am from a Christian background while my husband is Muslim. For reasons that I cannot tell he got me to be his wife. I think for them getting married with Christian and Islamize her is a kind of a great religious agenda. I did not know that and got married with him. You when I married him I lost all my family.

They all together excommunicated me for a simple reason that I got married to a Muslim man and of course a man from a different ethnic group. At first I didn't care much about it. I knew that it was the outcome of EPRDF's indoctrination. But as days go by it made me feel alone and just consider my husband the only creature I have in this planet earth. I got my first child from him five years ago. Nevertheless, after three years when she became a two years old kid he got died of AIDS."

Professor Jonathan is taken by panic. A lot questions are coming to his mind, in fact, without sufficient answer. "Is she getting crazy?" He austerely continued to gaze at her. Her tear drops are running down her face. "There must be something wrong with Eliza tonight." He moved a little bit away and started to pee. He poured out the wish he had kept for long in his waist. As a matter of fact he also felt that she might have given him the virus as well.

"Stupid, I shouldn't worry about it. I am here to test mortality. I have to die and by so doing go back home and start my life with the father again. I am that lost child; hope he would welcome me very well." He thought of himself and his destiny in depth. Professor, Jonathan believes that man is the only child of God. Before the creation of the world he believes man used to live with God. It is in attempt to become like God that man has been made pass the tribulation of life and finally test mortality. Unless though this process there would be no way for man to be clued-up likes his creator. That is why, he always say "Thanks to be Mother Eve, who dared to eat that fruit of knowledge, that way in fact one big step into this process of growing into the likeness of my father. He loves me, I too. I will be back well home, though too much lost in this world."

After a long chat with himself Professor Jonathan raised a question to her, saying "How do you come to know that he died of AIDS?"

"Well he had all the symptoms. In fact, he had never told me that he is HIV positive. Nevertheless, after his death I started to be sick and went for a VCT. It is by then that I came to realize that I am HIV positive. Believe me, I have never been on the bed for sex expect for my husband since I married him. In fact latter i.e. after his death I developed hatred to man in general and wanted to revenge as well. Then I went to a second man from whom I got my second daughter. Now sex is not line of attack against men but also a means of income to my household, though, it doesn't pay me enough to survive."

"Are your daughters HIV positive?"

"Yes" she responded and continued to tell more about her daughters "I have taken both of them for a blood test more than ones. And both of them are found to be HIV positive. I want to be healed, we want to be healed. I do not want to die leaving my children all alone for poverty and this world. My prayer quest to whoever can respond to is to cry is listen please listen and act. Please the whole world listens to us." Again she plunged into a marine of tears.

Professor Jonathan tried to cool her down in fact he hardly managed to do so. However, she was not able to continue with him to the bed. She was so depressed and with a very heavy heart. Hence, he was forced to leave her and continued his way across the darkness. All told, he has no destiny to reach at. Eliza looked at him from behind "what a fortune man!" she envied him.

"What a free person." She said. "He has nothing to be concerned about; nothing at all; this system has killed him alive. He has lost all his mindset totally. He knows nothing but drinking and sleeping everywhere and with everywoman that he got on his way on the road. It is his flesh that walks on the dust, perhaps knowing that it will go to be dust itself someday."

She was radically astonished for a while. "What a time, a university professor losing his human merit and acting as those perishing animals ...remarkable!" She accompanied him through the water of her eyes. As she got in she saw the coming generation already half bare and half boring. After a while she said "... then what will the future cling to?"

OUTSKIRTS OF LOVE

Kolfe is as usual very hectic, as busy as bees. People run her and there for meeting their goals in life. No one is static at all. Everybody works hard in Kolfe; otherwise one may get the basics of life at all. The problem is the village is not paying well as elsewhere in Ethiopia. Labor is cheaper than the cheapest. Life, on the contrary, is a little bit expensive. The work that eats up the whole day may not give money that may procure full bread. Anyway, people live, people move and people aspire and people die as well.

Mame Abera is among those running fast and hard to succeed the daily breads of her family. She was brought up with many other children together in her village, but of all Alemu is always craze about her. His love for her has its root while they were in elementary junior secondary school. "Whenever she used to associate herself with other boys my heart used to bump and my whole body used to be angry at her." This was what he replied to his father when he was asked about their relation sometimes ago.

They are very much concerned about him. They don't want him to marry her. "Listen my son, I sense the strength of love, and yet I don't want you to marry a daughter of a witch who can never tell who her father is. Don't be imprudent all in blood and flesh are not human beings, some of us could be devils incarnated in human skin."

"How come a human being can be a devil?"

"I can't reason out, but experience tells us so! From what I know we all were angles living with God, until God wanted us to come down to earth and pass through trials. Devil was one with us who wanted to take God's seat while we all wanted to continue to worship him."

"That is pure religion!"

"I know pure education can't go that far. You know what, science is also a logical religion based on findings, nothing more."

"You right, but at least science gives sense."

"You know don't be too proud for you have your first degree in Medicine, if you don't apply the wisdom you get from therein, it actually is nothing. You see the biggest university in this world is life and the best teacher ever witnessed is experience. Learn from us. She is a witch. You are a pure human being. How come a human being sleeps with a witch? On the top of this she is neither schooled nor cultured."

"I know the fact that she is not educated. It is because she is poor. Otherwise she is brilliant, we have been together up until she moved for vocational school. Otherwise she could be a medical doctor like your son, daddy."

"Above all she is dirt poor. It is always to die with the rich than to live with the poor. I don't want my son to be married to the poor and die while alive."

"Daddy, you might have truth in what you are telling me. Nevertheless, try to understand me my heart bets together with her heart. I love her. I can't live without her. Love is a wonderful institute, once you are in it, you can't be out." "What love are you talking about? There is nothing like that in the wake of EPRDF. Everybody is selfish, as an individual, as a family and as an ethnic group that is it. If we be large we can't make a country more than a tribe."

"That is EPRDF, father."

"Whatever, you can't marry somebody from next door. If you do there are your own people, your own tribe, your own blood, your own flesh, and your own bone. Didn't you know the first man ever married his own flesh, you can't be any different?"

"That is religion!"

"Well, if you can't live for my words as usual, surely I will kill both of you." He just can't forget this dialog which he had with his father long time ago. Since then he has stopped to meet her overtly.

Alemu is catching his 25th while she is just in her 21st recently making her certificate from a vocational school in kindergarten teaching. "It is by miracle that I reached this level. I wouldn't make this little achievement in my life, without the hidden support of Alemu in my school life. He is such a good person. He is the great one that I am indebted for. I could say he has raised me from the scratch and have developed me to this elevation. How can I run away from him Mammy?"

"I would love if you be together. That is a wonderful opportunity to my family. However, we are from the out caste group. As you well know the society has ex-communicated us.

They don't like to be together with us. They don't consider us a human being. I very much doubt his love and the consent of his parents towards your mirage with you. My daughter you love will fade. It really can grow old. And when it dies you will have a hard time with him."

"Now it is my turn to serve him, mammy. He has always been good to me. I have to come in his shoes and do the same for him mammy. If He dares to marry me, there is no doubt I will give him myself. He loves me and considers me his breath,"

"Are you going to leave your weedy mother and brother to hard time again?" Her mother exploded into tears. She felt so lonely and left aside even by her own daughter. Mame embraced and kissed her mamma clearing the tears running over her face but couldn't answer this question. She kept mum and continued to love her mother and care for her more.

Mame looks well groomed, today, Monday, January 2006. She is already out of home going for her school where she teaches the little ones. She saw people fighting for Taxi. She looked around and made sure that Alemu is not there and said' Thank you God that I have never ever been using Taxi." The school is a walking distance from home. She likes walking. She used to walk close to 6km a day to complete her vocational school. Not because she hates to use Taxi and/or other publican transpiration, but she didn't have enough to pay, sufficient to eat and adequate to relax by.

Today she has come out of home superbly decorated. She had fixed time to date Alemu. They will meet right after her school. Her red dress together with her fair-haired color has given her a glowing outer shell. Her straight nose that crosses her oval red face into two hemispheres is like an equator stopped by her lips that veil her snow colored tooth. Deep in the heart she has Alemu swimming in the ocean of love located in her tender heart.

It is 6:00 O'clock after noon. They look one body sting sleeping tighter in the Hotel. She is melting over his chest. He is trying to swallow her starting from the lip. The electrodes of love have connected them very well; no background, no color, nothing at all but Just love.

"Can I get in?"
"We can't do that before marriage?"
"I can't stand the volcano moving inside."
"You have to be a man of your words. Don't forget our promise." She felt cold down the heart. He has already released it. Immediately both plugged into the bath and started taking shower together.

Somehow they sit together in bath and started to warm one another naturally.
"Can't you tell me a little about your whole life?"
"What new can I tell you about myself? As you well know I am from a very poor family that leads life under destitution; a kind of malformed life that you can't find words and/or expressions strong enough to articulate it." Staying in silence for a while, Mame continued "We are just three: my mother, myself and my brother. You just can notice that my family is a kind of woman headed family. My mother is the maker of our life; she is everything that I and my brother could imagine in this shanty world of ours." He was eager to hear anything about what he has heard about his mother.

He wanted to ask her "Is your mother..." he ate his questions again and rose another question about her father "Isn't your father alive?" Instantaneously, her emotion exploded and she started weeping. She looked into my eyes through the water of her hot and red eyes and said "Don't be panic, I don't know my father. He deserted me and all his family when I was a five months old baby."

I said "Why?"

"It is a long story, my beloved one ... you see, my mother somehow came into personal relationship with the Lord Jesus and despite her poverty she acknowledged Him as her personal savior."

He interrupted her and said "... with Jesus?"

She replied "Yes with Jesus. And at one good night she wanted to witness the love of Jesus that has won her heart to my pitiable father and she did it that same night. Can you imagine what would his response to this wonderful good news of eternal value?"

He kept mum. He was not listing into her last words. He was pondering "A witch receiving Jesus as her personal savior. The two couldn't go together for him. "Well my father must have been wrong. Her mother is just a human being." He was clearing all his doubts from his mind. She didn't recognize this and all of a sudden, she paused her hiatus and continued "He bitten her brutally he pushed all of us out of home. Since then my mother rented a small room and managed to grow us earning below $0.5 a day through selling her labor worthless for the sake of me and my brother."

With a broken heart, he asked her "What does he do for life?"

"He can't read nor could he write; currently he is working as a daily laborer in a hotel around my village earring lesser than what my mother used to get a day. Had it not been for the intervention of God in my life, my fate wouldn't have been very different from the fate of my brother; to remain illiterate. Thank God, still he has one reason to live there is Jesus dwelling in his life. He has nothing; I am telling you what do three of us in my family have except for Jesus? ... Nothing, I tell you nothing."

She was taken deep into her own emotion. Her thought buried her inside. After a while he came in and asked her "How much do you love me darling, he started to lick her lips?" She just couldn't utter a ward. She simply responded by giving herself to him. Again in the bath they flew away to the other world: a world that knows no hatred, no disparity, no cheating, no pretence and acting.

"I love you."

"I love you, too."

"When will you marry me?" It took him time to respond to this question. It was his father's word that came right into his mind.

"If you can't live for my words as usual, surely I will kill both of you."

He took some time and said "I guess for us to be together, we need to flee from this country and seek for asylum where we can have freedom. This country never belongs to us. They don't understand us. They don't let us go our way. This is a country divided on the basis of ethnic background and religion. Thanks to EPRDF, we tend to hate each other more often than we can accept each other. We are highly divided, even disintegrated. You have seen many couples politically divorced. You know how many women are left single mother, for their husbands were deported from just being Eritrean. I mean this is a fucked up system. I tell you, they don't let us live and die our death... what not"

"Stop it!" She cried. Silence came in between them. Both kept quiet for a while and a bite latter saw each other in the water their tears. Both are crying; crying like a kid? They saw each other in the water of their tears. Love is keeping them connected. They warm up by each others' heat. They still suffer from the cold outside.

"It is magnificent, love is always wonderful. It has no boundary, at all. Love is the only innocent thing ever created in this world. I love it. I adore love itself." His mind was taking in stillness and amusement.

"Are you going to leave your weedy mother and brother to hard time again?"
The voice of her mother rebounded on her mid a number of times.
"Why going away?"
"My father will kill us. He is such an arrogant person. He never listens to others. Whatever he says is correct. Whatever he thinks is absolute. Whatever he does is perfect."
"So what?"
"He doesn't love you, my darling. He has warned me not be with you any more, my sweet love."
"Why? Is it because I am a poor?"

"No darling, he feels you are a witch."

She just couldn't believe her ears. Everything got upside down. She hated her being human. Straight away she jumped out of the bath put on her clothe. He tried t cool her down. But she was very thin-skinned on the issue that she couldn't listen to him. Eventually, she left him all alone in the bedroom and steeped out of the hotel.

He tried to dog her from behind like a small puppy. The moment he tries to catch her up, she is already gone. She is like a shadow, when approached she runs fast. However, hard he tried; he couldn't able to make it with her.

AMAZING PEOPLE

Haymanot Alemu came to my office early in the morning May 3, 2005 few days before the national election was conducted. I was reading my bible at John 1:1 which reads "In the beginning was the Word, and the Word was with God, and the Word was God." I was wondering how God's love impelled him to take action to help his creatures gone astray so when the time had fully come, God sent forth his Son, born of woman Jesus is the Son of God, the Second Person of the Trinity, who was sent for love of mankind. Hence, and I was bit spiritual and compassed by the spirit of the Lord.

She just knocked at the door of my cozy office. The office is just two by three but still looks very narrow. It has one big table with four guest chares and books shelve at my left. My lab top is right on the table. There are also a lot pictures and photographs of children everywhere on four the walls. All told, it is very calm and convenient for reading and writing as well.

She knocked again and I let her in. We greeted each other and she took a chair right in front of me. She brown blacks with long hair on the back falls a little bit below her shoulder. It is well combed and she is nicely dressed in white trousers and body. She has worn a dark balk glass and has carried a medium size bag.

"What can I do for?"

"Well I came from Sebeta." Sebeta is just 30km from Addis to the south west. It is small but busy town in the outskirt.

"That really good, by the way how is life there is Sebeta?"

"Good Sir."

I could sense that she is a little bit worried. Her face is now spiting sweat. I just couldn't understand the reason that has brought her to my office. I have never seen her before and neither did she, I guess.

"Are you a student in this university?"

"Yes sir I am doing my degree in Law?"

"That sounds great." She just was seating. I wasn't sure what to do for her.

Somehow, after a little break; I came again to ask her if there is anything I can do for her. Then only she started to tell me what has happened to her. She was broken but courageous as well. She looked hopeless but with good future as well. I mean she was a kind of paradox to me, a kind of thorny woman to value.

"If I am not taking you time, I wish if I start my story from my background."

"That sounds great" I replied.

"Will you have the time sir?"

I said "You don't worry you just keep on telling me I am ready to listen to your good story." Immediately she started narrating her story.

"By the time I was born, my father was a bank clerk, but when I was a 3 years baby he got dismissed from his job due to chronic disease and got to be a bed ridden one. And yet my family size has increased by three with my mother having given birth to two children: a baby he and a baby she. At this junction my mother went out to do anything she could to get money to feed the family and treat my father." I interrupted her and said "May I get you tea or coffee."

She said "I am fine" and continued her story.

"Very hardly, spending the whole day out of home, she used to get below 50 cents a day. All told, she was able to send me to school but very hardly. I used to go to the traditional school to learn reading and writing. I was just five years by then. That same year.." She said and paused for a while. She breathed long and took time, I guess to think, her words.

"I got stolen by people, whom I can't tell anything about them. These people took me to palace that I have never been to before." Now I am totally immersed. I have never heard people telling this type of story.

"So what happened then?"

"I was eager to hear deeper and wider about her."

"They pierced my eyes!" I shouted. She comes apart into tears. I looked at her eyes. They are covered with the dark black glass. Emotionally took the glass from her face. I couldn't believe my eyes. Both her eyes are blind. I cried again. We cried for a quarter of an hour. I left my seat and embraced her. She is just 17 years of age.

"When did this happen?"

"During this regime sir, I lost my sight and perspective. I lost my loving and caring parent; I lost my moral values and principles. This regime has messed up everybody." She screamed. Many losses, she uttered. I was scared, and yet I asked her to continue telling me what has happened to her then after.

"They made me beggary. I used to send the whole day begging and begging when it is about nightfall they used to take me home and take my money all. That way I spent, three years. One day I told my entire story to the person I was begging at a traffic stop light. He just couldn't believe me and asked me if I am willing to go with him. I responded yes. He took me the blind schools at Sebeta. It is last year that I joined this university. Now I am doing Law. I want to combat those people who put to this world of blindness."

"I asked her to tell me a little more about her childhood but she said "I don't want to recall those days of my life where my family was in an ocean of poverty. We had quite numberless days without enough food to eat. Many years have gone without proper clothing and medication."

She breathed long and said "If at all there is anything to fight against, it must be poverty. It can easily turn the man that God has honored into a vapor dust. What do you want to hear about this darkest face of life where there is no beam to hope for, where there is no power to pray for, where there is no one to look after for help? I tell you poverty can make you disgust your most loving God. I just don't want to say anything about it anymore and anytime." It looks that she is made up of even thinking about it anymore.

"We'll let us forget about it and come to what has brought you to my office."

"Well I need your help."

"Like what?"

"I am in trouble."

"My English Instructor under your department has raped me yesterday!"

"What?" I was panic. I just couldn't control myself.

"How was that? When was that? Who was that? ..." I poured a lot lead questions inadvertently.

"He summoned me to his office yesterday at about 6:00 in the afternoon. I went innocently hoping that he may want to assist me as a teacher. As we meet in his office he just told me a lot about his special heart to me as I am a blind student that may need special help from him and the rest of the community. He kindly informed me that he would like to introduce me with his wife and children so that I will have family of mine somehow he took me to his house. When we reached there was no body at home. Up until they come back home, he invited me for vine. We started taking, as it was a new experience to me, I got drunk after. In the morning when I was awakened, there was no one in the house. I just found myself raped on his bed."

"A university professor did this, Haymanot?"

"She said yes sir!" and she kept saying "Are you surprised the fact that how a professor did this sheet?" She laughed for a while. When she laughs she opens her mouth as if she is opening it for a dentist to pull out her last but resent teeth. She makes it a free and relaxed kind of mirth, not because she is that happy. However, the extreme side of grief is always phony cheerfulness.

"They are also victims of this regime. They are made out of mind too. Most of them drink alcohol to hide themselves from their mind. Some run away when they get the opportunity. Some prostitute themselves to hind asylum in the embrace of a third person. All told, they are damaged, by the politics of this country. They are reaped themselves well. Most of them are fucked up and they mess up the life of them students. On the top of that most of them are government gents. There are there not because they deserve, but because the ruling party wanted them to be."

He didn't want her to talk too much on the subject. Hence, he interrupted in an attempt to get her attention, "I am not surprised. But, wanted to know as to what measures did you take following the incident?" In fact, he was partially panic while trying to get her back to the point.

"I immediately went to the nearby police station and told the whole story to the police officer due for the time."

I interrupted her and said, "That is wonderful. What happened then?"

"The police officer replied that I am blackmailing his name."

"Whose name?"

"The name of the person who raped me"

"How come he said that?"

"He just told me that he is a respected member of the ruling party, and he felt that it is what the opposition party might have conspired against him to defile his name so that he may not win in the election four days ahead."

"Are you serious?"

"I swear to God!"

Without more ado, I fall on my knee and asked the Lord "Hasn't the time come for you to listen to the cry of your people?" She joined me in prayer and we spent almost the whole day supplicating before Him.

JAWS OF DEATH

A weak has gone since the May election has come to an end. The rumor has it that Ato Belete Gelmeso has won vote in Ambo, an old town to the west of Addis Ababa. Belete is just a security guard for the Ambo college of Agriculture. He is never educated but has a good public acceptance as he is a member of the oppositions party. He looks honest and hardworking. He is married to W/r Almnesh Gulate, 36 of years of age. They have two children and yet have no enough money to grow them properly.

Belete needs change. He is tired of the ruling party. He all the time says "I and Ambo frantically need a change. This broken single and old street must be multiplied. The only ground plus in the city has to be proliferated. I myself and people like me must get sufficient to live through hard work." He is very much optimistic. He imagines one day being a fabulous man in the city putting everything in order. "Now has come the time. We have won the vote. We will see what is going to happen." He speaks without fear with whom he meets everywhere in the city.

Today as unusual they have sat together attending a coffee ceremony in their neighboring compound. There are about five people attending the ceremony. Everybody sat around the coffee table which was as short as 2 inch above the ground. The coffee cups are escorted by stunning fragrance. The green grass which was put on the floor like a carpet gives the room an outdoor scenario.

All discuss about Belete's burnt residence. Alemnesh In fact, nobody knows who put it in fire. But, everybody knows who gave the firing order. The problem is they can't speak it out openly and loudly. They are never allowed to be loud on purpose. The freedom of expression, in the law is a just for law sake. The prime minster is the law, nothing more and nothing less.

"He doesn't listen at all. He has no ears, I believe, indeed! I mean who else has ears to listen? Nobody! We all are the reflection of the system. I have told him not to count against the ruling party. They are cruel. They can do anything they wish." One of them suddenly spoke out of anger.

"We don't have to submit all our life long."
"Belete they will kill you. These people have no excuse. Why don't you learn from the past? We have already lost out home and the possession we had therein. Is it not enough? Do you want them to kill you?"

"What if I die, it is for my country?'
"I need you Belete. My children need a father. I need a husband. Why should you die? Said Almnesh and slowly went long back in her thought may be recalling the trying time she

had gone through to bring up her children. She remained long and deep in her memory.

Belete was gazing at her in tears. It looks they have so much in common so to speak. One of the attendants interrupted their floating in thought and asked Belete "why are you weeping?" Trying to clean his face from the tears he said, "Well we have every reason to cry. If I start to tell you form our recently loss it was a last weak right after the election that they burnt our house entirely burnt to ash."

He took a long breath and continued to put his loss in the picture "Everything we had as a household was brunt just in an hour time. Just last week at about this time we were having lunch all together at home. Nevertheless, an hour latter i.e. at about 2:00 o'clock, we got every possession we have burnt. It is only me my children and my wife who were rescued safe from the fire." Again, he kept quite. His wife is still lamenting in silence.

But after a while "I tried, we tried, all tired to save some of my things but unfortunately all including my ox which I use for farming my land got scorched. Now, I am bare, poor. I have nothing to look at; no hope to aspire, not at all; except for the result of the election."

"The result of the election can't be a home." One of them mocked. The rest were in pity tyranny. Some even have plunged into an ocean of tear for some time. The mocker himself was strongly touched by their situation, but wanted to make a kind of comic relief. Suddenly, one of them asked "Where are you living now?" Almnesh said pointing at a tent made from plastic" in this tent which our neighbors for us."

"Do the local governors know about it?"

"Yes, they do." she said.

"What action have they taken to help you in this regard?" another person asked after finishing the coffee in his cup.

"Celebration! They celebrated the incident. They burnt my house and feasted their pleasure." Almnesh interrupted and said "Ato Belete, we have lost the house already. Please take care of yourself. Do not talk anything against them. I am saying they will kill you."

The coffee maker has sat behind the coffee table which was decorated by green grass lied on the ground, a traditional charcoal stove-top behind and a black pot full of coffee on the stove. Somehow she took the chance and started to say "We all are poor. Most of us are poor farmers. If you take my income, it is not more than 1200KG of grain per annum. We don't eat three times a day as many others in the compound. We eat two times a day for the majority of our days and there are days where we have nothing to eat and go sleep with drinking water only. Our food items are always one type and hence they are not nutrient. We live in a village where we can hardly grow a child. I mean children die mostly from poor nutrition and water related illness. We have also mountain malaria."

Taking a little time to inhale she continued to tell about some of the major problems in the community "we don't have enough school, and clinic in my village. Most of us are poor to the extent that we do not have enough to eat at times. And yet none of us have come against the ruling party. Not because they are good to us, but we fear them. As you they jail without reason. They kill without law. How can one stand them in the wake of their cruelty? Belete you are never right to join the opposition party, what so ever. I am really very worried that they may kill you if you don't resign very soon."

Soon after she poured out coffee in all cups ad distributed them all to the attendants, including Belete, who what not that happy in the ceremony. One of them who claim to be a fortuneteller finished drinking his up and ordered the coffee maker to burn incense. Now the hose got full of smock but with special fragrant aroma. The man looked into the cup trying to read from the remnant vestige of the coffee he drank. "I tell you Belete, today is not your day. This adversary will not stop without killing you. I see the fire that burnt your house, burring the whole body of yours." Everybody heard the words of the seer critically. But Belete did not give him his ears.

All started to talk to each other on the statement of the soothsayer. The discussion went on. One of them started to lobby Belete "You see if you betray them and join the ruling party. I am sure many will follow your foot print and even the local governor will rebuild your house. They even may give you a better job, who can tell?"

All of a sudden Alemitu fall on the feet of her husband and crying loud beseeching him to resign and join the ruling party. "I can't do that" said Ato Belete. "I shall. How many times will I die if they kill me? Is it not only ones? I can't surrender any more. I can't do such a stupid thing in my life." He continued shouting.

In no time three armed cadres surrounded the house. Ato Belete was told that he was under arrest. They took him to the nearby jail. Alemity accompanied him in tears. His children were behind her following the foot prints of their father. After a while a gun blast was heard, it was Belete who was shot died just on the cross road.

FAKE FREEDOM

It is 7:00 in the morning. Some selected political hostages were told to join the mass in the small hall near the meal house. No one has a slightest idea of what is going on there. "Why are they pushing us to the hall?" they just murmur. Some say "May be they want to free us." These spy prisoners are secret agents of the ruling party kept in the prison for exceptional assignment. They always trigger discussion and then focus listening to others. Nobody knows them very well. They are like wolves in sheep's skin.

Most of the prisoners are quite silent. Over the years, they have come to realize the fact that speaking free in the prison is not safe. Still were others talking good and bad, some verbally and some through their eyes and gestures. Some were praying deep in the heart for good thing to happen.

"Nobody can tell the heart of this regime. They may finish us all in the hall and tell to the public a bomb has exploded in the prison." Nearly all of them looked at him in panic. He has been in the prison for more that sixteen years since the inception of the opposition parties in the country. He is the pioneer of one of the parties in the nation.

"Don't stare at me. I just said in my heart. I can't trust them, period! They are snakes in the grass. You never see them coming. You only know when they crunch into your body, that is what they are. What else can they do on a human being like me than torturing me for over sixteen years now without law?" He is just shouting like a barking dog.

"… killing, let them do it now. I prefer death than such a life in the top-security prison. I have never been allowed to see my family for long. I can't recall the face of my wife. I just can't bear in mind the voice of my children. I am exceedingly excommunicated. I have never seen the human right people coming to this prison, never at all. Is that humanity? Should all of us think the one and the same? Are we identical products of a given factory? God has created us all in His own image but with a lot of varieties. Why can't they understand this? Why don't they see in the beauty that could come out of diversity?"

His hot and red tears tag along his talking. Everybody nodded down and shaded tears with him. Instantly, two police men came and vehemently took him away. "As usually they will pack him in that small room." One of them said in the heart. "How could they let him join us today? He has always been alone. Even they don't let him come to the meal house. They used to take his meals and waters to him themselves." others murmured. "He is already crazy. He was just a brilliant one years back. How many have gone mad this way Oh good God?" one tried to show the harm on His workmanships to God.

Bite by bite the small hall in the jail strangely got to be full of prisoners. The person in charge of the prison came to the pulpit and said "Good morning all, I guess most of you do not know the reason why we are all here. In this present day, we have a visitor from the government. He has a message to share with you. It is my belief that the guest will be around very soon."

People started to mumble again. "Who could it be? What message? Why with us? ..." A lot of questions came into the whisper. But nobody was able to answer any of them. One of those wolves said "May be they want to continue political discussion with us on the points of our differences?"

"How come they have this heart?" The other one replied. "I am relay bothered, what else can it be then?" "They may also draw our life to a close, who knows? As they were taking on their wild guess the said guest came in. He is well dressed in double button suit. His shoes look either new or well shined. Sooner, the head of the prison invited him to the pulpit.

"Dear friends, good morning to all of you and greetings from the standing government." Nobody responded in any way what so ever.

"As you well know but only too little, Ethiopia is entering into a new Millennium. For this reason, the government would like to free you all of any charge for the swift approaching millennium provided that you will never be involved in the politics of this country as opposition party, any more."

The whole house murmured, but in resistance. As soon as the delegate fished his speech one of the wolves raised his hand for complimentary. "Dear prisoners, you know we have missed one great opportunity of participating in the parliament and even governing the city of Addis Ababa. That is a great mistake, I guess. If we were in that position today, we would have contributed a great deal in the development endeavor of the nation. But that is gone.

We have already missed it. This is another great chance to have a kind of contribution. It is always good to be free than to be under captivity for anything to come. Hence, I gently ask for us all to think of this great opportunity and say Amen to the invitation."

The house whispered again in conflict to what has been said. One matured mild professor raised his hand from the corner. The state delegate saw him and said "In fact I am not here to facilitate discussion. I want to hear just your opinion to the matter and I will go back to the government with that. On my part I did not image any opposition on this cream idea. Any ways let me listen to you and with that we shall wind up."

"Thank you so much for this great opportunity" said the professor in a dying voice. He looks to be severely tortured and mal treated. "For me it is a wonderful idea to think positive to us to be together with you to celebrate the overhanging Millennium. I am grateful to you on that."

The sate delegate smiled at the confusion of the house. Nobody has expected professor to come to say that smooth to the ruling party. "Is he going to submit? What does he mean? He must have become tired of this penitentiary life." Some have discussed softly their guess to their own mind.

After a while, professor continued "However, one thing that you are missing understand is the passion as well as the position of the Ethiopian people towards this political fixture. Where are the public masses?" he again paused.

He again continued after short leap. "Are they with you ready for celebration or they are with us here in the prison? I tell you we carry deep in our hearts the great and horned people of the nation. They are all incarcerated with us. Go and look for the mark on the public, the mark of every hit on our back, the mark of every punch on our face. Our pain is their pain and their pain is ours. They are all with us. Can't you see their hearts locked up with us in this hall? We all are imprisoned in this small jail, or in the nation as a whole." The house puts hands together for the professor.

"And yet, if you are talking about this false freedom of yours…" he continued "…we are already free with the people of Ethiopia. We are taking pleasure in the spirit of independence that they enjoy outside this campus. That is where lies the mystery of our being together in the great jail of the nation."

The tone of his speech has improved radically.

"I tell you, you can't free us keeping the public in custody either you do free them without getting us out of this course, thank you for listening, your honor!"

The house put hands together for him once again in a higher degree and superior passion. Nevertheless, he didn't sit down to welcome the appreciation. As soon as he finished his last word, he started going out of the house for good. Many went out after him.

FINGERLESS FAMILY

I was born into a family of nine children as the eighth child. I have three sisters and five brothers. In fact, my father who was a farmer in a little farmland in my village was while alive. He died from a kind of disease that could have been cured if he could have enough money at the time of his illness. My mother, on the other hand, suffers from leprosy, as my father used to do.

"When did you acquire this disease Mammy?"

"Some twelve years ago"

"Couldn't you mange to see a doctor?"

"My some the nearby clinic by then was as far as a three days walk for my place."

"If you had the interest, that was no that far compared to the damage that the disease has cost you and your family, today?"

"Well, I had no idea about its after effects."

"How come Mammy, this ruling party is very much concerned to the farmers, didn't they take the pony to create awareness in the village?" I mocked.

"Are they concerned?" She also mocked and said "I have never seen that in my days thus far. If they had any concern for people like us they wouldn't have damped us over here in this desert."

It was people suffering from leprosy who established the village, where I was born and brought up. These people have migrated from various places in Ethiopia in an attempt to go away from their own community that excommunicated them simply because they have the said leprosy problem.

The village has only one small clinic and junior secondary school. There is no single high school in the area. Hence, the fate of all students in the village after completing their junior secondary school is just to stop their study if they are able to go to the hard by towns to pursue their studies.

My father used to take me to the nearby mountain and used to pin point at the other mountain far ahead with his fingerless arm and ask me to see far-flung.
"Can you see the green grass after that mountain?"
"No daddy"
"You must be able to see my child. I f you only see what is around you cannot go beyond the limit and achieve in life. You must be able to see. You don't have to look around. You don't have to see your situation. Be a man that sees far ahead."

I used to strictly follow his advice and do hard on my study. Hence, academically, I was among the very few victorious students in my school. The tragedy started after my going to Adama the nearby town to perusal my high school study. Somehow I fall in love with one of the beautiful ladies among my class mates. She doesn't know where I came from.

"Well what matters most is our affiliation. If we really love one other, game over. Our parents could have no greater say than you and me."

"Are you serious? I hearted you father is such a strong man."

"Never, it is just because he is one of the cadres of the ruling party. As you well know people don't like such politically active community members."

"If you are a daughter of a cadre then you are a princes."

"How came you say that?"

"Because they can do whatever they wish."

"How?"

"Forget that and let's take about our own headache? Do you think they will love me as your boyfriend?"

"Sure.''

"I swear to God, what can they say if I really love you deep in the heart."

"How about the forthcoming child, will they welcome it?"

"Well they don't have one. They should like it. But my father these days is gravely asking about it. I guess he might have suspected my pregnancy."

"Are you serious?"

"By the way how about your parents; can your parents have a strong say?"

"I can't say."

"Why?"

"Well, I don't have parents at all?"

"Have they died?"

"Well, can't we talk about something else?"

Whenever we discuss about family issue, I just will shrink and lose were to tread at. My fear is what will happen if she comes to know that I am from a leopard family?

"I am she will hate me?" "
No she can't do it."
"How can she do that?
"Is love such a simple thing?"
"If she does this, she must be a carry woman?"
"Why don't I tell her the truth and see what may come?'
"What do I mean? If she sees my mother she will never see
me again. We are marginalized people. Disregard individuals,
the regime doesn't mind about us."
"Any ways she is already pregnant. Hating me would mean
hating her child."
"What if she aborts it?"
"No, no she can't have the mind?"

I spent the whole night without sleep discussing with
myself about her. I brushed my tooth, washed my face and left
home for school early in the morning. Sadly, she hasn't come to
school today. I tried to find her out by eyes. She wasn't around.
I wanted to get to class but I just couldn't do it. The question
"Have she aborted the child?" came into my mind. I just
couldn't get rest at all.

"If she knows my background she could do that, but if
otherwise she can't do it. Her family needs a child. They have
no other child except for her." I decided to go to her residence
and see what is up with her.

As soon as I reached there I get filled with a special courage
to knock at her gate. They opened the house I asked them about
Suzy, they said she is sick. I told them that I am her classmate.
"Are you Alemayehu?"
"I said, yes with a smiling face."
"Come in please."

I guess she is her mother. She didn't take me direct into the room where she has slept; instead I was taken into one of the service rooms. She let me sit down and started asking me questions.

"Is she your girl friend?"

After a lot of struggles I said "Yes, she is."

"Do you have sexual relation?"

"Have she said anything about it?" I answered the question by asking another question.

"Forget here. Now she is in a serious trouble."

"What is new?"

"She had an attempt to make abortion and she was about to die."

I just couldn't believe my ears. "Are you serious?"

"Was it from you?'

"What are you talking about?"

"Was the pregnancy from you? Bull sheet! Can't you understand?"

She started to be angry on me. Following her shout her father came in and said "Is he the one?

She nodded "yes". He did not have the patience to solicit any more questions. He just jumped over me and spent the whole day hitting and biting me. At about noon I was almost out of mind but was able to ask the reason for these all hitting.

"Could it be because of this untimely pregnancy?"

"No, it can't be?"

"Well, could be because I am from a fingerless family?"

"No, it can't be. How could they come to know my background?"

I raised many questions and answered many "NO"s. The only thing that I came to understand very well after a long time is my fathers' advice. It flashed back time and again in the back of my mind.

"You must be able to see my child. I f you only see what is around you cannot go beyond the limit and achieve in life. You must be able to see. You don't have to look around. You don't have to see your situation. Be a man that sees far ahead."

"Yes" I said to myself I have been short sited. I should be strong and do a lot in education to change myself and the situation of my family. I somehow made an oath inside my heart. I felt as if this woman is not going to be mine, unless if I don't want to die.

Now I wanted to b released from their captivity. They kept me the whole day without food. It is now approaching sundown. No one is coming to where I am. But from a near distance I hear somebody digging a ditch. I was so hungry and so tired and about to fall but some a voice crossed my ear; "What a man that never knows who he is! How can he dare to sleep with my child having known who he is?"

I came to be sure that this family is annoyed about me. I also came to realize that they have known my background very well. That even could be the reason for the abortion. I wanted to get out of the room. They have locked me from behind. I tried to scream but no one is responding to my cry. After some hours her father came back again with a pistol at his hand. As he opened the house, he just asked me a couple of questions.
"Are you Alemayehu Abera from Tesfa Hiwot?"
I said "Yes"
"Is this child from you?"

I kept quite. He asked me close to three times. I didn't hear his voice any more but I saw fire coming out from the revolver towards me.

TOWARDS MISERY

Mulu Gojam was busy doing her everyday routine by the time she went to her Beauty Salon to talk to her about her current life situation but I tolerated enough till she could have enough time that she could spend with me. Nevertheless, when the due time comes i.e. after seeing one of her clients off, she welcomed him in and started telling him her career since childhood.

"I am the only daughter of my father whom I lost when I was a little one. In fact, I have never known my mother since my childhood. It was my step mother whom I used to confuse with my biological mother, as I had no information about her whom I finally discovered to be dead while my age counts at months below zero years of age. In fact I have some siblings two-three in number from my mother (step one)."

He looks listening to her but in actual fact he was gazing at the ins and outs of the salon. "It is very crazy and I wondered why many prefer to come here?"

He just could not get answer to his question from the outset by gazing what in the salon. It is as normal salon as anyone else. There was nothing special in it. Just as usual beauty salon as always is. Even those beautiful ladies who were like the smiles of the house were not there, for some reason. Just the two only were walking tenderly on the squashy street of that soft fantasy world.

"There are hair conditioners, next to them the big wall glass, and then the big white shelve with the comb in it, the hair cutting equipments, the shampoos and the lotions are arranged over it and some hair styles on the walls. Oh sorry, I forgot the sofas chairs and washing and drying machines."

Nevertheless, all together couldn't tell him anything about the secret of her being preferred in particular by ladies from the opposition group. He had no other options that listening to her words and, hence, he turned his ears on her lips.

"In fact, at that moment of my childhood whoever was able to give me food used to be my mother. This was so because I almost lost my biological father before I became five. Hence, I was almost a parentless child left with step parents who couldn't care about me. There, I had to fight my level best to get my everyday meal and virtually my clothing as well from any one on the street. I was somebody like a street girl." She was breasted into tears. Her eyes and her heart were weeping together.

It just couldn't give him sense. But she just continued to narrate her story as it comes to the lips. Deep in her heart, she has a belief that he has to know her from the scratch so that things will not panic him as they go deep into the world of love.

"If you ask me about how poor we were, I assure you that I can't tell it in terms of human language. Leave alone me; just a human being with a lot of limitations, angles can't explain it as it is true to my level of understanding. We were extremely meager. Our daily issue was our daily bread that was it!"

She just went off and wasn't with him for some time. When she got back from her deep thought, she continued to say "But what surprises me, when I think of my life back, is that Jesus never forsake you whatever poor you may be. He was always with us. When we didn't have anything to eat He was there with us to suffer hunger with us, when we had nothing to wear He was not ashamed of being the member of our family. Our home was His home; He was the head of that poor family."

She is not coming to the point where he wanted to take her to. She is going astray, deliberately or otherwise. He felt like directing her to the gist of his yearning. However, she could not give him enough time to drive her that opposite direction to her destiny. She just continued going round the bush.

"My step-mother was a strong Christian. She had a well-built love to Jesus, in fact she had no one else who could take her closer to himself and talk to her the things of her heart expect for Jesus. She was by herself to the majority of her life than not. However, she had never been pity. She was always strong and high spirited."

"Were you good at your school? I mean where you an average student or better?" he asked as a starting point towards his goal. His questions were escorted by his obsequious smile. He just flashed his pasty white tooth and covered them with his smoldered lips by the smoke from his everyday cigarettes.

"No I wasn't. I had a lot of problems. Being poor for a woman like me is really so difficult to bear. I just couldn't stand the feeling of being underprivileged that used to emanate from within just deep down in my heart and became competent enough in my academic life. I just couldn't go beyond elementary level of study. I had the opportunity but I just couldn't."

"Do you have a room for a man to get into your heart?" Now he got almost to the center of the ocean.

"Well, I just can't say anything now and yet I don't really want to push a frank man away."

He laughed deep inside and "I am afraid you are doing exactly what you dread not to do."

"You mean you are honest."

"Time will prove that for you. However to start with I want to give you a tender kiss. Can I do that?"

He closed the gate and just jumped onto her lips. They eat each other's lips. She was utterly faint. He was almost without breath. Both of them were gasping their last gulp of air. Somehow, he pulled out his back tong as a snake is coming out of its cave and started to lick the tips of her breast. When he moves his tong between her two her breasts, it looks a red snake is moving on her chest down to the heart.

Both of them were too hot to reason out. He was totally lost. As he went on fire trying to make love with her, she almost finished the path without letting him deep into her. She had already flashed out. On the contrary he was driving himself extremely crazy towards her. As he was trying to put off her pants, she came back to sense and said "No, we can't go that far at ones. Give me enough time to ponder about it."

She pushed him back towards the wall. Struggling with his libido which is about to over flow like molten rock, he said "Well for me it is a very good beginning. As of now, I would thing I am engaged."

"Well, that sounds great." She replied.

"By the way can you let me know one of your clients, Kebebush? I like her argument as member of the opposition party. Is she a lawyer?

"Sure, why do you want to get to know to her?"

"No if I am gonna be your boy friend, I have the moral obligation to protect you and your loved ones."

"What do you mean?"

"You see, I have heard that she they are going to arrest her very soon."

"Are you serious?"

"I am telling you."

"So what is better?"

"Give her call and let's date her somewhere and discuss the solution together. Let me take you two, for dinner to Sheble Hotel"

She, right away, gave her a call and asked her to come to the Shebele hotel to be together for dinner. "Well she will be there after two hours at about 9:00PM in the evening."

"That is great. By the way do you have a restroom?"

"She answered "no."

'Well let me rest somewhere and will be back in five minutes time."

"Fine" He let her for the rest room.

"I got her." He felt as if he is a superman. He gave a call to his boss and told where they can find Kekebebush, tonight.

"She is a resource person. I will trap all the rest using this woman as a means."

After a while he returned back to the Salon. She welcomed him with a smiling face. He pretended his smirk and kissed her and sat down. A moment latter kebebush called.

"Mulu, thank you for the dinner, tonight I am not going to be out."

"Why?"

"I can't tell you the reason by phone. We will meet any time in the future." She hung up.

"Was it Kebebbush?"

"Yes"

"My goodness," he went out again and gave a call.

Kebebush is strong politician, a persuasive speaker, a woman of strength and courage. She is exceptionally gifted at argument handling and debate procession. She has ideas after ideas. She has established herself in the public debate screened through the national television. Everybody has appreciated her talent of dispute along with the good words she uses. She is like spire on the chest from the ruling part. They don't like her potency of words. Of all they are very much concerned about her unrestricted public support. She is also a woman of love. She loves and respects her husband who supports her struggle against the ruling party. However, she has one weak spot. She likes alcohol. Ones she starts drinking she will drink it to the last.

"Well she has canceled her program."

"Do not go for that. We much be able to trap her tonight. I have already fixed camera on table 17. Room 203 and 204 are made ready. Hers will be 204. It is there that I made the cameras fixed."

"You know what I am saying?"

"Yes, but I don't want to pay attention to it. You must get her into the trap tonight. By the way do you have enough money at hand? "

"I have 10,000.00ETB"

"You can make use of it and give us victory tonight."

As soon as he is done with the telephone dialogue, he went back to Mulu.

"Where did you go?"

"I am not feeling healthy today. I guess have some bacterial infection."

"Are you sure?"

"I tell you."

"If that is the case, Kekebush was right to cancel the dinner party."

"No, I can't accept it. Tonight as we enter into this special world of love, we should start it in such a way that it can never be forgotten. On my part, I have this present for you." He gave her the 10,000.00ETB and embraced her and moved around her lips. Mulu couldn't believe the incident.

"What is this all money?

"My gift for you"

"This much money?"

"Forget it; I am going to give you myself. Now give a call to kebebush again and let's be together at a dinner banquet here in this beautiful hotel where angles sit together to enjoy life with devils. Hope you will be able to invite us."

Mulu took the money to her bag and called kebbebush again. "Tonight is a special night in my life. As you are the most important person in my life who helped me reach this height. I want to have the pleasure of you company to the dinner party I have arranged to my boy friend. It is only you whom I want to introduce him to as my family."

"Well I just don't want to stay long. I will be there after an hour. Pick me from the gate of the hotel to your particular tablet."

Mulu and Solomon left the Salon soon. As thyme reached to the Hotel he drove to table 17. When it is time for Kebebush to arrive Mulu went down stairs to receive her from the gate. Before their arrival he ordered a bottle of Whisky with three glasses to drink it with.

"This is my boyfriend."
"My name is Kebebush."
"Nice to meet you Kebebush" They shacked hands and sat around the table. After a brief chat, the table got served in the restaurant. It looks the hotel is well informed about the matter. Their alcoholic beverages followed the dinner.

After a while the second bottle came. Three of them are now a bit into the mood. Mulu has almost lost control of herself. Solomon is not that very bad. He is all right. Kebebush is very hot. She smokes and takes the alcoholic imbibe as if she is drinking water. After a while she also got lost. Solomon drove her to the room prepared for her to play the rest of the drama. He left her there and went to the next room to enjoy Mulu.

When it is morning, a video film was on in both rooms that demonstrate their terrible night. There was the seventh man with pistol sleeping with Kebebush. She saw how crazy she was the whole night. She also saw the other six gangsters who raped her the whole night while she was out of mind.

She cried and cursed the date. "It has already happened. The only chance you have afterwards is to publicly reject you party and join ours. If not we will make this craze film public so that the public know you better in this setting as they do in the other milieu as well."

It was clear for her that he was talking about the political dispute forum she had with the top officials of EPRDF as grounding for the 2005 national election. She cried deep. He lighted at her a lot.

"It is the work of Berket." She impulsively shouted. "He is bitter than a biting snake. When he can't win me on the right battle field he brought me to this butchery center." Tell him that killing is not winning."

They guy continued to snicker. She was like wishing the date of her death. At one hand she wanted him to kill her, at another, she thought of her loving spouse and children. She stayed like for two hours in tears and deep sorrow. Finally, she asked him not to make the video public. He shouted "BINGO".

Mulu was also howling in the other room. She just hated herself and despised humanity in general. Deep in the heart she has decided to commit suicide.

"I wish if I were dead today." She cursed the days of her life.
"But you are alive." The seventh guy to fuck her mocked.
"Can I have my time?"
"Why not? But I want you to answer my request first."

"Please leave me alone."

"You leave us alone, too."

"The game is over man. Now I want you to give me time to lament my shock."

"You see EPRDF is always smart." He ridiculed her.

GOOD COMPANION

Mahilet Lemesa, is currently living with her grand mama. She is indeed a beautiful young woman with a brown chocolate color, only 13 years old. Despite her being fine looking, she does not odor to be in good health and cheers. She has a broken heart, a heavy spirit and dying flesh.

In short, as an author I just could not read a sense of optimism on her face. She is quite wrecked to the extent that she does not want to talk about any part of her life with any human being around. She wants to be alone and by herself always. Hence, I had to ask for her consent even to talk to her about her own life affairs.

"Do you really allow me to have interview with you?" I just solicited for permission. She immediately answered my question with another question saying "About what?" as if she does not know why I am there with her. We already had fixed a long time appointment with her for succinct interview about her life demonstrations. "About your own life witness; would not you love to share your life testimony with me and with our readers?" I again raised the question to make sure that she is happy with the interview.

"That is fine. But you authors do play a lot with words. I don't want you to exaggerate me in your painting. I wish rather if you don't take my picture by the camera of your pen" She dozed off. Her oval face has started to wide smile. By some means, it even became circle expanding sideways.

My inside whispered, "This must be a sign of acceptance from deep within."

I nodded to "yes" to the voice and smiled to get her into a right frame of mind for my talk with her.

"Sure, if you are not happy about it, I would not do it. I assure you I will not take your picture and nor I will use any one of your pictures from our document to back up this story. Trust me; I will never do that breaching your consent. Even so, do you mind if I ask you why? I mean, can you explain me your reason for not allowing me to take your picture." She again smiled. This smirk, however, does not show pleasure exploring from the deep in the heart.

When she said, "That is fine. I trust you!" I just felt a sense of a very great responsibility. However, now I was a bite confused even not to continue with the interview as well, thinking that she may not want others to know about her HIV status. "Are you really happy to continue with the discussion?" I asked her for the third time. She nodded "Yes" and started to explain me the reason why she does not want her picture to go with this dialogue.

"Well you see our society is not good enough in handling people like me who are living with HIV. They spot at you as if you are a different creature. They look at you as a person that has been cursed and punished by God for your cumulated sins. They do not want to touch your fingerer. No one welcomes you, whatsoever, no body, I tell you. You know what has pushed my mother out of home?"

Somehow a kind of deep thought took her away from our tender discussion. She started pondering about her most loved mother. I could common sense that she was heavyhearted. She started sinking deep into the grave of her heartrending memory. In an attempt to get her back to the discussion I said, "No, would you mind sharing that story with me?" She was very away. She heard none of my words. I had to speak a bit louder to get her back into the mood. "Are you with me?" She said "Yes" as if she is getting out from her nap and started to narrate her story.

"You know ..." she took her time and continued "... my grand mama had no peace with her first husband from whom she got my mother. They used to quarrel and fight almost every night. They had never gone to bed in cheers for love. He used to hit her, insult her and disregard her. Hence, she had to divorce him and get married to another man. By then she had three children from the gone man already; one among them is my precious mother." Again, she kept tight-lipped for a while.

"Was your grand mama contented with her second husband?" I asked.

"Never at all, she never had a peace with him as well. As before, she dejected with him. He used to thrash her and do anything awful in the planet earth to afflict her and make her life downhearted."

95

"Why?" I interrupted her. "Don't ask me such questions." She laughed and continued" Eventually, she was compelled to divorce him and started to be a woman of many husbands as that woman in John chapter 4. You understand me?"

"Yes I do." Now she is living with alone. I mean there is no man in the house as a husband even though many come and go."

"Surprising!"

"No it is not. The problem is with our men. They cannot handle their women as expected. They hammer them as they desire. They do not regard them as human beings. They do not perceive them as their equals. They do not have values to them." After a while, she continued to give me a kind of advice on behalf of the men. "You see, you need to do away with this rubbish culture. You need to love your wives as commanded by God. It is bad to hate your woman. The consequence is always dangers. It may go even beyond divorce. It has claimed the life of my mother."

I suddenly interrupted and asked her "How?"

"Well, my mother was a fine looking young woman. She was good in her education. However, she had no peace of mind with her family. She used to be disturbed by the everyday fight of her man and dad. Finally, she got tired of it and left the house. Unfortunately, she conceived me from a man that I do not yet know as a father. Then, she was compelled to drop her school. Well, after my birth, she had to prostitute to get many to grow me well. Eventually, she contracted AIDS."

"Okay" was the only word that came out of my mouth. However, she went on to tell me the story in more depth. "Well, people came to know that she is HIV positive and they used to spot her as a cursed woman. Everybody started to talk about her. As a final point, she left the village and disappeared. Now no one knows where she had gone to. She has disappeared for ones and all."

"How come, leaving her only daughter alone?" I asked her being fully in panic.

"Well, the society has tormented her more than she could put up with. She was highly stigmatized; totally excommunicated only because she has the virus in her blood. There was no single person in this world that used to give her love. She had no friend but me. All told, she could not put up with the excommunication and finally vanished as I told you to a place unknown to me and my grand mama."

Thought, she does not feel very much anguished, I just could not stand the misfortune of her mother in the story. I struggled with my tears. I started to implore for the futurity of her mother and herself. "God hear to the voice of this little kid." My inside pleaded to her. With a very great fear, "Have you ever cheeked your HIV status?" I asked her.

"Sure, I did a couple of times." She responded to my question so swiftly and plunged into unusual type of laughter. It was not only laugher; drops of tear were also rolling on her face. I saw both tooth and eyes depicting the tragedy of being distress together for the first time. It was not difficult for me to calculate the result of the test, but I wanted to give her the chance to tell it out herself. "What was the result?" my heart started running in my chest. My heat has increased. I was almost full of anxiety to hear the result, though already have guessed what it would be. She took quite a long time to answer my question.

I just could not believe the wind that carried the statement "I was found positive." She shouted. I shouted. I just could not continue any more. I failed on the knee, started crying about this little kid before God. As I prayed, I could sense how much, our off-putting cultures as mistreatment of wives, marriage harassment and unnecessary stigmatization could turn one's life to dust.

THE HOWLING CHILD

Addis is so frosty today. Everybody curiously feels cold. These days the weather is changing a lot. It has become strangely bitterly; may be because of the unexpected waft wind from the Indian Ocean. Unlike the other days of the week, it is so chilly that it does not encourage one to get out of bed and go out for even work. On the other hand, the road is jumped. It appears that everybody is marching to all directions in the city to attain their daily routines.

Somehow, she took taxi to Ato Gemechu Wako residence. "Everything is changing. All our values have gone. We are under cultural colony these days. We are invaded without our knowledge. There is no honest man, there is not honoring man, there in humble man, there is no ..." In my taxi, the man who sat at my said after a brief gesture with me but not with warm greetings as common in the traditions.

"What do you mean?"

"Can't you see the weather?" he replied. Nonetheless, she could read his mind that he was trying to comment on my style of greetings. She did not hang on him, which she had to do it as per the tradition. "Sorry for not greeting you well." she apologized.

"It is okay, everything has gone with the weather." He saw a sense of forgiving her not for the small offense she committed. "I think, unconsciously, I have hurtled you, I apologize again." She begged for mercy yet once more.

"Don't cry over spited milk, lady!" he shouted. She sensed a sagacity of unwillingness to forgive her. She was not surprised by his answer, nor was she was broken by its tone. She was well aware that forgiving is one of the things that the society has dropped over times in her culture. Even in the church, it is hard to go between two people for reconciliation as well as forgiveness. She wanted my discussion with him, any ways, but she could not. She has arrived where she was destined to—the residence of Ato Gemechu Wako.

The weather has continued to be even colder than before as it was starting to rain. Be that as it may, many are on the road rushing to meet their headache for the day. Ato Gemechu, however, is at home, waiting for her coming to converse with her about his personal life matters.

It was a week ago that he fixed an appointment with her at his own home at this hour of the day. She rushed early in the morning to his house, thinking that he may forget her time with him and leave the home early in the break of day.

She has heard many saying "Africans have too much time in a day, may be over 24hrs that they are so much extravagant in using it their time the way they are expected." In other words, we do not have enough work to keep us full of activities all the hours in the day. It looks life is too long to most of the Africans to live as never has been else where in the world despite short life expectance rate in the country.

"Good morning Ato Gemechu" she said.
"Good morning lady!" He replied.

Despite the weather, he feels very well today. She also greeted his two children. One of them is called Ramsa Gemechu. He is quite a young boy in a good spirit but not with a joyful face. He looks calm down all the time. It seems he does not have the freedom to speak in the wake of his parents. That is how it is in many of the places in Ethiopia.

"Children are children." Many tend to say. Briefly, what they say is they are not matured and nothing good can come out of them. To put it differently, they are not expected to do great things in their society, never at all.

"How are you doing Ramsa?" Ramsa looked into the eyes of his father seeking for permission to respond to her question. "Well praise be to the Lord, we all are just fine." He responded after having the say-so from his father.

"Have you taken breakfast?" Ramsa's mother asked her after warm greetings.
"Sure" she gave her short and succinct answer.

Her intention was to serve her with what is available at home. Eating and living together is one of the strongest sides the culture around Addis. Everybody likes to share what is available. The lifestyle is not individualistic but together and by so doing enjoy life together. The problem is when it comes to work. Please find it difficult to work together.

She did not listen to her while responding to her invitation for breakfast. She continued making the table ready for banquet. Immediately, she brought some loafs of bread with coups of tea. She did everything herself; no one helped her either in preparing or in arranging the food for us. In my fellow citizens, boys do not go to kitchen for preparing food, what so ever.

All house courses are racially the jobs of woman, even if they have productive works out doors. In other words, even if their spouses are ideal in the home all the hours of the day, they do not go to the guts of helping the woman in the housework. However, these days, this is also changing with the weather.

Boys have started going to kitchen preparing food and assisting their life mates. In fact, it is just on the start.

All gathered around the table and closed their eyes to praise the lord for the food and the day. Ato Gemechu praised the lord and we all opened our eyes to start eating. Now we are only three around the table. The two children were not their.

"Where have they gone? Why don't they join us in the food?" She asked.

"No, they are children. They cannot sit together with their parents. They have to wait up until we finish eating. It is only when we terminate that they can sit for the food to eat the ruminants" said Ato Gemechu.

She was not surprised with the answer. It is her culture. It has grown her up. The culture works with children away from the substance. It does not give due place to them. They cannot sit down together with elderly ones for anything worth of relationship, not at all. In a way, they are abandoned. They do not participate in decision-makings, even on their own affair. Children are deprived of their rights and dues.

Right away, she recalled in her mined the man that she met in her taxi on her way to Ato Gemechu'a residence, who said, "Everything has changed!..."

Yes, many things have changed. We are losing the good things we had and now we are full of what is radish! ... Where are we going? What is the matter? What is going on?... Who is responsible? Who cares for this nation? ..." She shouted round the bend.

CEASELESS TEARS

It is a small cozy room. Tomas Tolosa and Elzabet Melkamu reside in it together with their fine-looking daughter, Jemanesh Kebede. The house is a kind of bed-sting room, where the kitchen, the living room, the bedroom, the restroom all together happen to be mixed up in a miniature spot of land. There is only one single bed and a kind of undersized bench made from dry wood in the room.

In fact, the bed is curtained to panel it from the rest of the spaces in the house which is used as a living room and kitchen in the day hours and bedroom in the evening for Jemanesh who sleep on the floor over peewee maters.

Without exaggeration, the house doesn't cover a total area of more than 10 Squares Metter but still it is comfy as the family managed to maintain love and regard to each other despite their adversary.

The two couples are in their 10th year adversary of matrimony. No one is invited and nothing is prepared. Just three of them are together at home conversing the essence of true love and enjoying the pick of life.

"You remember How we mange to make marriage?" Tomas with a kind of heavyhearted fortitude said "It was ten years. Well it was me who initiated love to grow deep into the soft soils of our hearts, I guess"

"That is true." Elza replied.

"How about your Mammy, didn't you have any role in constructing this wonderful love."

"I did."

"What was your role then?"

"Welcoming your beloved father into my heart"

"By then, both of us had no other enemy than poverty. We were hale and hearty. We used to look like colorful fishes swimming in the warm pond of life and love baby" said Tomas stirring the tender hair of his daughter.

"But we had love. If you have love you feel as if you have everything in this world and the world to come."

"That is wonderful. But what do you mean by love?" Jemanesh loves to ask questions. She is a cute kid truing t her fourth years of age.

"Well we used to love each other. We had a special affection to one another. We were and still are devoted to one another. In short, we used to have joy in each other's charisma." Jemanesh interrupted him and asked "How about now?"

"Now..." he kept tight-lipped. It looks as if he was rewinding all the walks of his life that he has gone from beginning to now with his beloved wife across the grueling path of days.

He continued to say "Now, when I look back into the beginning and all my way till date, I thank God, we were able to get married and manage to be together despite the adversaries and have you Eliza." He again paused his speech for a while and started clearing the tear drops from his eyes.

"Both of us are trustworthy to our life together. I have never known a woman except her and either did she. When I married her I gave myself to her ones and for all. That same day I felt receiving my wife as a special gift from God above. I always feel in this world there is none other created for me. On the top of that we used to take care of ourselves." He again kept unspoken for while.

Eliza took the chance from him and started to philosophize. "In this sort of developing country, ones care alone can't help that strong. People need to put hands and heads together for common goals and interests. There has to be ethical and disciplined sort of people everywhere. Democracy, good governance, honesty, dignity to man, integrity, excellence, these and other values we need to build up on. Our self care and hard work would be a futile exercise."

Latter on Tomas came in t speak touching his cute daughter at the head he uttered "I tell you Jemy, for us, we will continue to live together till death does part us but …" He somehow pitched into shedding tears. His wife interrupted him and asked "Why are you so worried about her Tommy? Why don't you leave her for God?" It took no time for him to respond to her question "I don't know Elzi, but I at times feel as if we, their parents, are not blessed with long life span." His speech was escorted by his tears. Eliza could not stand hearing him saying this. Though she is not speaking a single word she already was in tears for a while. Jemaesh could not understand what is going on. As she saw both her parents sobbing she also joined them in weeping.

"Would God be looking into our tears and respond to our special quest of healing?" Tomas asked himself in stillness but it was just a question, his inside wishing the power of God clearing the virus from their blood.

It seems that all the three were looking into each other's future through the water of their eyes. In fact, it was like as if they were doing a farewell salute to each other's heart as they may not be all together living under the same roof after a short while due to the killing virus fastening the pace of the death in the body of the two couples.

It was four years ago that Eliza contracted the virus at her delivery table.

"The table was full of blood. I was told by the nurse to slouch down of it. I begged her not to be on that table. But she insisted. I can't forget what she just said on that curial moment."

"This is not a private clinic. If you want safety you have to pay money. This is a free government hospital and has to accept whatever is made available for you."

"As she was speaking hard, the childe came out. That moment, I had no other option than reclining on the table or else the child will fall on to the ground and may die at birth. It is her carelessness that has caused me to catch the various. ... to save my daughter I risked my life and the life of my husband."

FLYING AWAY

"Thirty-nine people who had been stranded for days in the Gulf of Aden between Somalia and Yemen were rescued Wednesday by a Danish vessel. They are the lucky ones among the rising wave of illegal migrants from the Horn of Africa who make the perilous journey to Yemen and other Middle Eastern countries to escape violence at home and seek a better life elsewhere."

Mamush couldn't believe my eyes reading this page from the internet. He got to be a little barmy. "What is going on?" He asked himself. His eyes got to be watery. He threw his cigarette down to the dust. "The whole Africa is flying away." He cried deep in the heart and continued to read.

"The crew of a Danish vessel Wednesday spotted the 39 people waving frantically from aboard a small, rickety boat foundering in the Gulf of Aden. They were dehydrated and exhausted. One died shortly after the rescue, and one woman had given birth the day before, United Nations officials say. They are part of a massive wave of migration from the poor, conflict-ridden areas of eastern Africa to the oil-rich countries of the Middle East and on to Europe."

Without his wits he summoned the other man who sat at his left in the internet cafe and said "Have you read this news please?" "Which one are you talking about?" The man wasn't so clear about the question, he wanted to read and then comment.

"This article" he just pin pointed on the screen and said "Is it not amazing?"

The man skimmed the two paragraph which reads as "Spokeswoman for the U.N. refugee agency Mr. So and so says, using ancient trade routes along Africa's Indian Ocean coast to the Gulf of Aden, on average 100 people a day arrive on the shores of Yemen during the calm-water months of September through March.."

"There are a lot of Somalis and Ethiopians that have come across: Somalis most likely from the situation in their country, the lawlessness there," said Ms. So and so "Ethiopians might be going because of finding economic opportunities. Part of them is economic migrants and trying to use these routes to reach that goal. And crossing oceans is never easy and getting access to countries is never easy. But people take the risks and pay thousands and thousands of dollars trying to try to find a better life, risking their lives especially in this part of the world. It's a two-day journey across rough waters infested by sharks, pirates and unscrupulous smugglers.""

"Why are they flying away risking their lives to death?" He asked him back. "What do I know? Most of them could be looking a better life for their children, especially as Africa appears to be losing ground in its effort to raise standards of living. They are escaping joblessness, oppressive governments, lawlessness and starvation. I guess."

"Do you know these asylum seekers are an easy victim for the smugglers in the area?" Mamush kept mum. His brother has left home three weeks back to cross the same ocean to run away from the ruling party in the country who seek to put him to jail only for his sound difference in his political opinion.

"Can't you read over here, this week alone, smugglers ordered at gunpoint 369 Somalis and Ethiopians onboard four motorized boats to jump into the water and swim ashore? They were about six kilometers from the coast. Only 50 people made it to shore alive and were taken to a camp in Yemen run by the UN agency for refugees. The bodies of another 75 were recovered."

He paraphrased the whole paragraph in brief. However, Mamush doesn't look listening to him. All of a sudden his eyes released galloons of tears. No sound, no cry but drops of tears crossed his face. The guy was worried.

"What is wrong man?" "Nothing,…nothing at all." Mamush cleared the tear drops from his face and continued reading the article.

""In March, at least 90 people, including women and children, drowned when their boat sank in the Gulf of Aden not long after leaving the Somali port town of Bossaso, a major hub for illegal migration. Three people survived, some badly beaten. Two days later, another 85 people were ordered to jump overboard once their boat neared the Yemeni coast. Of that group, 18 of them drowned. These are among the recent incidents that have been reported, usually by the survivors themselves. But U.N. spokeswoman Ms. So and So says most deaths at sea go unreported.""

All of a sudden Mamush shouted in tears "My brother must have died. I have seen a dream last week. My dream is true. I have seen, somebody coming and taking both of us to the jail. That jail is his grave and that person is this incident… " He was speaking out of mind trying even to interpret what he saw in the trance. Ones again his eyes poured out rain of tears. The guy has understood him now. Fortunately, there was no other person in the cafe.

"Has your brother gone away in this root betraying his country?" "When did he do that and why did he do it?" "Just three weeks back because he hates this government" "What was his name?" "Are you his brother?" Mamush answered each and every one the questions he asked him. What he thought of the man is completely different. He contemplated the fact that this man is so concerned wanting to give a hand to him, nothing else.

The story was different. In the end, the man came out with his natural color. He pulled his ID from his chest pocket and showed him who he was.

"They are everywhere." Mamush whispered in the heart.

Putting his ID back into his pocket, the secret agent said "You're under arrest." The tone of his voice is totally changed. It is heavy-handed and overbearing as well.

"I know." He replied. He just couldn't say anything more.

"Go ahead." He packed him in the car and took him where he wanted.

VANISHING IN A JAIL

The pressure and the intimidation reached its climax on the 2nd day of January 2007, following my spiritual teaching for Christian University students in the church around Entoto. In the late afternoon hours I was conducting a sermon on the story of Daniel reading Daniel's chapter 6.

The gist of the teaching was, therefore, "It is good at times to say 'No' to the Kings and 'Yes' to the will of the Lord." and discussed with them what the will of the Lord is for Ethiopia and what the standing ruling party is saying about it. A lot of emotions and a lot of ideas were reflected in the meeting.

However, that same day when it was close to 8:00PM, two guys wearing the uniform of the Police stopped me from driving and told me that I am under arrest. I was shocked and asked "why?" Nobody could try to reason out. They had no care for my questions as always for others questions as well.

Right away, they took me out of my car and packed me in their vehicle, covered my eyes and ordered me to lay on the back bench on my chest. I did as told. After an hour drive, we reached to a place I have never seen before.

"Get into this room."

"I have a diabetic problem. I can't stay away from my tabs. I am under medication... I take 3 tables of Glibeclamide and 2 tables of Metformin HCL 500mg" I cried.

One of the shouted "Get in!" The other one hit me on the head.

Their hard words pushed me in. I got into the room, where I was stacked and kept for a day and half without food and medicine.

I cried again asking for mercy.

They kicked me in from behind and said "We want your death."

The room they put me in has no light. It was made from mud. The ground is not cemented instead it was full of dusts and pests. I felt as if I was put into my grave alive. I spent those hard hours in tears, crying before the Lord for mercy again.

On the following day no one has come. No food and nothing. It was me and me alone. In fact the pests were there some of them feeding on me and the rest of them playing their games on my body.

After the 2nd day nearly after lunch time both of them came to my room. They had strong sticks and their pistols at their side. I felt as if that is the last day of my life. I lost confidence. I did not know what to do. I was already tired. I didn't eat for the last day or so neither could I had my tablets. One of them jumped over my left leg and stood over it. He was trying to mix it to the dust. I can't tell how painful to me and pleasing to him

The other one flagged me with his stick from behind. I just couldn't cry or scream. I had no enough power to do so. I was already starved and made unwell. I was already done. So far I had no idea why they are doing such inhuman act against me. I have never been to the court. Even I wasn't sure as to who these people were except for their uniform.

"Will you stop your evils against this government or not?' one of them shouted, I kept mum for one thing the question wasn't clear to me for another I was so tired due to my diabetic problem and couldn't even say a word.

The other one pulled me up. I barely stood. "Why don't you respond?" he asked me and pulled his pistol. I felt he is going to finish me and made a kind of word to my Lord "Receive my soul, oh Lord!' deep inside. Instantaneously, he kicked me on my forehead at about my let eye by the back side of his gun.

Following the punch my face was covered by blood. My body dropped down on to the ground. As I was falling, the other one beat me with his shoes just around my right leg near my knee. Both of them left me in the room bleeding. Somehow I struggled to stop my bleeding using the dust on the ground.

At last I managed to survive. After some hour, when it was about 9:00PM in the evening, both of them came back, I guess to see whether I am still breathing or not. By the grace of the lord and His might I was alive.

"Hay man listen to me carefully, this is your last most chance. If you continue to write anything against the government or agitate people to revolt against the ruling party, be it in the church compound where you meet university students clandestinely or elsewhere, surely you will be killed and your family will be subject for torture.

That is all; the ball is in your court. If you still want to play with the fire, you do it and will harvest death out of it. Bull sheet! Okay!!!" He shouted and forced me to singe on a paper that says I am willing to be killed if found writing anything or speaking against the ruling class.

After my signature he pulled out his pistol. Then, I only heard two three bullets fired up. In a moment I wasn't any more.

LIFE IN JET-BLACK

"It is hope that keeps you strong!" said Lema Megersa, quite a young boy approaching his 12 years of age but with a lot imaginary lines on the bottomless contemplation, while he started his narration about his life. It looks as if he has many questions in life.

Torment and torture have already eaten up his heart. His spirit looks sternly affected. I wanted to know how and when and asked him to tell me a little about himself and his life situation, but he jumped into telling me about the death incidents of his parents with hot tears dunging over his babyish but afflicted fascia.

"It was two years ago that my darling dad left me for good." He breathed long and deep. "Well he was so ill. He used to loss weight almost on everyday basis. I used to think that this was so because we are poor and have no enough to eat. Nevertheless, the truth was different. I came to know the reason after a year or so." For awhile was totally lost. He just couldn't stand speaking about his incident in life.

"He died almost bare bones. With the help of many people in my village, my mother had tried to take him to hospital but he was never recovering. Rather, my mother herself started loosing weight. At first, I just was not able to believe my eyes. However, latter I sense it that it is true, my mother is getting slim, I wondered why? In the end, I convinced my self that it is because of my father's situation, because she used to be worried too much. Nonetheless, her problem continued to be worsened even after the bereavement of my father."

He paused for a bit and kept on uttering, "The neighboring compound took her to the hospital, where my father was taken and died. The doctor after asking her history recommended a blood test."

He really went away and yet his tears were dropping down like a minute brook flowing down the mountain. I myself could not believe the situation. I have never seen a person flying away far in contemplation and yet slashing in tears like this. After a while, he got back and continued to tell the story.

"It was AIDS."

Now he came apart in crying and sobbing. I was worried what to do. I prayed for a while but could not stop him from weeping. I cried with him. We saw in each other scratch. I could not stand looking at him as I saw him through the water of my eyes and plunged into tears again.

"Well to make the long story short ...," he said as if he is not interested to speak any more about his grief. "... My mother dead from AIDS just into two years time after the death of my father. Then after, our house got to be filled by darkness. Hopelessness and haplessness governed it all. Both of my parents left me alone for ever with my grand papa and mama."

After a brief silence, he continued saying "The tragedy is not yet over. My youngest sister went to bed yet again from HIV infection which she contracted from my mother. I had to help her in all her needs together with my ground papa and mama. As the assistance I used to get from compassion wasn't enough to help the whole family, I used to go looking for a job as a daily laborer to get more money to keep the family going well to survive."

I interrupted him and got him back to the situation of his sister "Well, she just couldn't stay long. In a year time, she passed away." again he took deep breathing. "As usual we buried her in the church yard where my parents were buried. The crushing hands of death could not come to completion with her in my house. My grand mama got sick, may be due to the strong pressure caused by the anguish. She just could not stay sick as my parents. She left me for good in two months time since she got under par."

I just wanted to swing the sound from this strong tragic tyranny and asked him a question "How is your life today?" This time he laughed. I was perplexed with his hilarity. Soon drop of tears followed his laughter. Now I came to know what his amusement means.

"Well I am not bad. I live with my grand papa. I am fine, fine with God. Though lonely in life, God lives with me in my everyday existence. God is my comforter. He is my shepherd;

I get everything I need for life from Him. At present, I am finishing my elementary level of study. I am looking forward to join my junior secondary school next year."

I instantly recalled the fact that this child is just one among the many children already subjected for street life due to AIDS. "Who is going to take care of these children? Who will shape up their future?" I asked myself and ponder a lot.

THE SOBBING DOG

Her eyes were hot and red, but still tearless. The scroll of her tears was dropping into the bottom of her heart. Tensely, she sat down on the edge of the hole dug in the bedroom for David'S burial. Her month was shut as if determined not to be opened any more, any time and any were.

She started staring at her life form the womb to the tomb. "A long way to go," she spoke to herself. Then, she looked at the lines at her narrow square palms as if scared of her own fate. They were as red as crimson. Hot blood was gushing out from them. Clotted blood has covered everything around her. Let alone her palms; the bed the mattress on the floor, the graduation gowns on then beside … what not!

The world was full of fear and tear. The king of darkness was baptizing the whole nation in the blood of its own children. "It is revolution", a strong voice penetrated the roof at once. Chachi looked up the ceiling. There was nothing around.

That same voice shouting: "Yes, it is a revolution; and revolution knows no mercy. If need be, it eats its own children" came down way to Chachi's attention again "What is it?"

Chachi asked her inside. The voice was piercing and yet it couldn't reach Hana. She was complete eaten up by her deep thought; her spirit was wondering away searching for peace and love all over the world.

That restless dog was watching her with a broken heart. It was sobbing in silence. Hana looked down at the dog. They saw each other through their tears. She saw love and faithfulness inside Chachi's eyes.

"What can your faithfulness do in this shanty world, Chachi?" The dog understood her question before it came out of her mouth "Yes, she is quite right," said Chachi "I couldn't even stop those demons from damaging the family." Something came and took its words and drove her to the memory of events there days back. Everything crossed its mind. Laughter and tear got mixed in the nucleus of her heart. It plunged into untold anguish.

"Cry not Chichi Cry not?"

"Why not Hanny? Why not? ..."

"Why sobbing, Chachi? There is no revolution in your small world Chachi." Both were able to hear each other's internal voice

"Can you see, Chachi,, what a revolution does?" said Hana, pointing one 0f her fingers to the bed and the other one to her pussy. Immediately, the last man who raped her after three young soldiers came in to her vision. He was the one who killed her lover before he threw himself on to her cooling his heat.

"Hana was quickened with the voice, and saw up on to the bed. Her blood-soaked eyes fell on David's chest. It is both swelling and graying. "He pierced the nucleus of my love with his bullet," she burst into tears again. She couldn't control herself.

"For heaven's sake, bury me soon."

"How can I bury you? How can I do that? Form where can I get the courage?" Immediately, she stood up on to her feet and took two fast steps to the bed. Chachi was following her by its tear-filled eyes. She added two more steps as she reached to the bed, looked into the wounds made by the bullets. At same time, she saw the Macarov that the terrorist left in the bed as he was on the heat. "Bullshit" she breathed long and swallowed all her tears into her belly. She saw his eyes; they were melting in to their own howls. His skin had started changing its color to gray. All his body had grown amorphous. Despite these all, she embraced him and kissed those dead lips. "Dave, take me! Take me, too. Leave me not, leave me not alone".

As her eyes were raining scrolls of tears, her voice became stronger and more perspective. The spear of tears, her voice became stronger and more perspective. The spear of deep anguish crossed her heart again. She became divided so much between love and fear that at times her inside forces her to commit suicide and at times her fear…" she said. Her laughter followed her tears. The dark shadow had started creeping across her life.

"Everything is finished; every hope is killed," she laughed and cried. She looked down at the dog. Chachi was still gazing at her. They saw each other again through their tears. "Chichi, will you be my witness… Something came and took her words; her own soul ate her up, gnawed her inside. "I never heard love to call my own, I was about to give up and you came alone. Hurry, what you need, I need you for always. Make me yours, make me yours make me yours, make me yours make me yours."

The song he used to sing to her while having perambulation across the fresh air on Bole Street, rang in her mind. "Where is that courage today, Dave? I can't live without you, Dave?" She plastered her soft and living lips on his dead ones, again. She ate up the feelings bottled up in her inside, the bubbling volcano just below her heart. She embraced him warmly. "Oh, leave me not alone; still support me and comfort me." The tears coming out of her tragic eyes were hot. "Woo, woo," Chichi interrupted her. "What is the matter?"

Hana asked immediately, she heard footsteps out side the house. Chachi continued barking and sobbing as the foot step was coming closer. Hana took the pistol. "We shall go together," she said and kissed hiss lifeless lips for the last It took her no time to pull him down to the grave and embrace his neck. She lay beside him waiting for anyone to come in.

"Bum...bum...bum"

The door got broken after a strong and recurrent aggressive push. It was that same person who entered first; others dogged him from behind for raping and stealing again. Right away, she shot him at the middle of his heart, and took the same cup and slept forever beside her lover.

"What a shanty world "said Chachi plunging into its own tears.

SUCCESS PINS

About the end of his 17th, there graduated from one of the High schools in Addis, a young man from a poor and infinitesimal family. His school record was good. He has scored eight "A's and only one 'B' out of his nine subjects in his high school leaving national examination.

Many talk about his excellence in his academics around his school. His ambition, coupled with a laudable desire to succeed, had buoyed up his strength until the final graduation day from his high school had passed. John Tsadiku is cute, superbly crafted child of God. He has all the determination to be somebody special to his country and the whole of humanity very soon.

After warm greetings, I invited him to take a seat on my guest chair. He did and started to look at the pictures on the walls. My office is snug and full of pictures and schedules on the wall. "Well your wall tells that you are working for people like us." Said Cherinet alter observing what was around in the office. "Sure, it has too. It is your office and has to smell your odor." I replied. He laughed. Bit by bit I took his attention to the first questions I wanted to raise for him "How do you see life in poverty? How does it feel to you?" He breathed deep and long. It seems that he has a lot to talk about the question.

"In the Old Testament we are told that when the Israelites journeyed through the desert, they were hungered, and that God sent manna down out of the heavens. There was enough for all of them and they all took it and were relieved. Suppose that the desert had been held as private property; suppose that one of the Israelites had a square mile, and another one had twenty square miles, and another one had a hundred square miles, and the great majority of the Israelites did not have enough to set the soles of their feet upon, which they could call their own. What would become of the manna? What good would manna have done to the majority?" He then kept quite. I also kept silent. We stayed in hush for some time.

Then he came in "Not a whit. Though God had sent down manna enough for all, that manna would have been the property of the landholders; they would have employed some of the others perhaps, to gather it up into heaps for them, and would have sold it to their hungry brethren." He again kept mum for a while and said, "You know what I want to mean?"

I said "Not really"

"Well, I want to be thankful to God as a whole for sharing that manna with us for free. I tell you, many have gathered that manna and have kept it at their bank while there are many of us dying out of poverty. Had it not been for God the Almighty, my fate would have been death as many other children in the world. However, thank God, I am alive today, for I could have access to this manna.

It is just my heavenly manna. It has given me that eternal bread. It has helped me to have access to Jesus, understand him well and create a good fellowship with him. Jesus is my friend, man! I love him; he loves me, that is all. Hence, all my success in life is connected to my relation to him in deed." He praised God in tongues for some time. I felt I am in a prayer room of a revived Pentecostal church.

"Sorry, that is my story: parsing the Lord for His priceless gift Jesus Christ. You know I was born into a family of ten people. I am the fourth child of seven children in the family. I tell you my family is a poor family, poorer than the standard set by the World Bank perhaps. They have no enough food to eat, no good close to wear, no enough money to go to school, no capacity to see a doctor while being sick… so many 'no's. In other words, they are denied of a very good access to that Mannna. However, we have one thing great in my family and that is Jesus but that is not enough. We lack the other three relationships. We are not well related to ourselves, others and the environment, by large." Suddenly he stopped his philosophy and started to gaze at me.

"All of us are in Christ. Hence, he gives us a peaces that many can't buy, he gives us a joy that many cant afford to buy, he gives us his presence in our family which we can't buy it by money even if we ere richer than the world most affluent man. In short, we have the manna but not to the fullest. You know for me this manna is all about relationship. If you be good with God and bad to the other three i.e. self, others and environment, what would it do for you?"

It looks as if he is preaching me about Jesus and relationship. He so emotional and so involved. The love of God is bubbling out from deep with in. I could see how much he loves Jesus and believes in good relationship. He is still ready to speak about Jesus. He is filled with the worship of Jesus. However, I wanted to divert him to the things I wanted to talk with him. "That is really inspiring. I can see what that manna is doing in your family. However, just to be to the point would you please tell me a little about your academic success? How do you come to score 8 "A" out of nine courses?" I asked.

"Your question would have been just the opposite. How could the one "B" dared to come to me? My brother, I am a friend of Jesus. It is He who gave me this success and will continue to bless me with wonderful achievements. He has given me the gut to study, the understanding, and the power to comprehend. He has the created the mind nicer than the nicest in this world, man. However, take care it is not because I study hard that I am successful. Instead, it is because He has a plan in my life and He is preparing me to that plan in my life. He will grow me. Now I will join my college preparation school. I will be successful there as well. Then I will Join University. There also I will be successful. Then I will go for my post graduate studies there also I will be successful?"

He paused and stayed in silence. I myself was taken by surprises. The way he speaks is so different. John came in and said, "Ask me why?"

He continued to answer his own question. "The answer is clear." He said. "The story maker is mine. The success maker is my friend. Jesus is there in my life now and He will be with me in the future. I live in him and he lives in me, that is all. If I be poor, he is in me. I do not want to think about my poverty.

Rather I would like to work harder on building my relation with the other three. Of all, there is a greater king in my life who can give me the manna even in the wilderness."

POVERTY IN THE US

On the 20th of March 2007, Maryland was chilly as usual. The summer has not yet started to manifest. When it was about 4:00 O'clock in the morning I met with my interviewee at the intermediate care unit in the Holy Cross Hospital, one of the most esteemed Hospitals in the area.

After warm greetings and some good words between us I explained her, the purpose of the interview and I continued with my questions following her willingness and endorsement for the interview. My first cycle questions focused on her personal date, such as name, age and marital status.

Answering to these questions, she said, "Well my name is Daniels Tomas. I am turning to my 78. My husband left this world for good, three years back due to heart attack. Since then I live in a single house. I am a retired staff of Hilton Hotel after 45 years of service as a secretary."

After taking notes of the information above, I took her to my second questions. "Why did you come to this hospital?" Right away she started to say "I was brought up to the emergency department by one of my relative due a non-stop vomiting and abdominal pain."

Her medical history exhibits the fact that she has a high blood pressure, cholesterol, chronic obstructive of pulmonary disease and acute depression. Due to such illnesses and the pressures resulting from old age, she is not able to perform household tasks independently.

"I feet fatigue when I get up and start cleaning the house. I cannot wash my clothes in the laundry; as a result, I ended up wearing my dirty cloth over and over" she said.

"Don't you have somebody like your relative around you to assist you in your household tasks?" I asked her with a spirit of a great enthusiasm. She appears very unhygienic with a terrible odor.

"My eldest daughter lives around my home, thought, she just could not lend her hand to me with all her three children at home. I have been paying four hundred dollars a week for some one to help me at home during day hours. However hard I hate it, these days, I don't think I am able to spend even a minute without a caregiver around me." After pause for a while, she added "I would rather prefer to die than staying long in the hands of caregiver."

My third question was to know whether she has medical insurances of otherwise. "I have Medicare part A and B and Blue cross Blue shield insurance. Part "A" Medicare insurance covers my acute care hospitalization while part "B" Medicare my expenses for doctor visit and physical medicine such as physical therapy and occupational therapy as well as my disbursement for my medical equipment. My Blue Cross Blue Shield, on the other hand, covers the bill that is not covered by both the part "A" and ""B" Medicare.

However, as I can't afford to pay the premium for my insurance and the co-payment for doctor visit, I have decided to cancel my Blue Cross Blue Shield insurance on April, 2007. By the way I get social Security income that helps me cover all my living cost."

Then I asked her he she saves money somehow for her other needs of life. "I would like to save some money to hire a live-in person at her house. I do not want to ask my children to pay for me. I want them to live their own life and I will manage my life. I have lived mine and I have to die my death alone." Immediately she continued talking about her prescribed medication cost without me asking her a single question about it.

"I pay for prescribed medication out of my pocket; therefore, she decided to shift to herbal remedies a complimentary therapy. The herbal remedies are much cheaper than the prescribed medication and do not have such strong adverse effects."

She only takes one prescribed medication for her anxiety which she could not remember the name of the drug. Since part D Medicare does not cover for herbal remedies, she decided not to apply for the benefit. It would have been nice if her family explain to her the importance of prescribed medication.

As I was concluding my chat with her, she started putting herself into bottomless thoughts. Immediately, she jumped into an ocean of tears. I could sense a kind of hot feeling which was bubbling inside. "I do not deserve to be here, why I am not eligible for home care aide?"

All of a sudden she became hyperventilated. I called the staff for assistance and I left the room.

STRUGGLE WITH DEATH

Mick Derege is a young looking wonderful man who aspires to be somebody that can stretch his hands forward to raise deprived people from the dust they are thrown to by the cured hands of poverty. He is tall and very eye-catching. He is now turning to his 21. As a boy grown in poverty he has a strong detestation to it and has personal philosophy about it.

"Poverty is the wildest enemy man can ever have. I have seen that animal myself and have been combating against it all my life long now" said Mick and soon after his tears exploded. As he was weeping, I could sense a kind of hot emotion blowing up from deep within. His face was turned red burned by the hot volcano coming from inside. He just couldn't stand his emotion for a while, which was telling a lot about how shockingly poverty has affected and afflicted him and his family.

Mick used to live in Addis Ababa in a small room packed with the rest of his seven family members before he joined the school of Law in Haromaya University. After a while he managed somehow and continued his talk "You see…" a little pause and cleaned up his face "A mother is a gift from God above."

He again paused and I simple continued observing what was happening there. "Had it not been for my mother, by now I would have been turned to dust, just below my own grave yard while having lots of wishes and hopes to support!" Again, he paused for the third time.

Mick was diagnosed to have smeared positive pulmonary tuberculosis and he was started on tuberculosis drugs. After he completed the full 8 months course of TB treatment he had no improvement and he was checked again. The sputum examination at that time, after he completed treatment, showed that he was again smear positive.

He was then put on the re-treatment regimen with the same drugs, according to the national tuberculosis treatment protocol.

After three months of the re-treatment, the sputum examination was found to be positive again. Sputum culture and sensitivity test was ordered and the sputum culture was also positive for the TB bacilli and sensitivity tests done showed that the bacilli are resistant to rifampcine, isoniazide, ethambutol and streptomycin.

At that point, the only option he had was to take the second line anti tuberculosis drugs, which were not available in the country. Even if the drugs were available elsewhere, it was not affordable.

"I have never thought such a challenge would come against me. However, it has, and the only option I have is to face the blow of fatality, just to go for good to the heavens while I have many dreams to accomplish on this earth." He was just hoping for death.

His treating physician gave him the prescription for the second line anti-tuberculosis drugs and he brought it to the attention of the Mamma. She had no money to buy the medicine, what so ever. "Poverty is going take my child." She cried. Her family is a female headed family. She lost her most loving husband eight years ago only due to a similar disease.

"By then also I weren't able to buy the drug and as a result I gave my beloved husband to the cruel mouth of death. Now the something is going to happen, I guess." She talks without someone to listen to her. Everywhere she goes she speaks all alone. When she comes to home she never dares to look at Mick with her full eyes.

Since the death of her husband, she brought all her children working almost for over 16 hours a day for insignificant pay. However, she had a strong hope on Mick that he would assist her to grow his brothers and sisters after graduation, provided that God would give him a job.

She posted a "Help me" notice everywhere. She broadcasted the same. Nevertheless, no one was willing to give her a penny. On the other hand, the health condition of Mick was going down the hill. He was having massive haemoptysis (blood spitting).

She used to spend the whole night praying for healing, but nothing has happened so far. There is no priest that hasn't prayed for. There is no church that she hasn't taken him to for healing. There is no witch that hasn't given him a traditional medicine. Still and all Mick'e situation was not improving.

He has lost over 60% of his weight. When seen in the sheet, it doesn't look that there is somebody inside. It has been close to one solid year since he withdrew from school by the time he was told to have multi-drug resistant tuberculosis. He has lost his memory entirely. He has become a bed-ridden patient. He spends all his time at home day in and day out under the good care of his mother.

At one night she prayed till midnight and slept. Suddenly, he started to gasp. She just couldn't help. She shouted. The entire next-door people came for help. Some joined the mother in tears. Some wanted to call for ambulance. Still were some who were gossiping about Mick saying that "It must be AIDS."

In few minutes time the ambulance arrived. Two people went to the bed to carry him out. One of them suddenly said "He has expired." The other one checked his breathy, temperature as well as heartbeat. Finally, he looked into his eyes. There is no life in them.

"He has gone." He screamed.

FANTASY MISSION

On September 12, 1986, I was given a kind of "run of the mill" mission of executing a cold blood assassination against Hutu' leader Didas Gahigy in Rwanda. The then command of the state in my nation coveted Gahigy be killed to end the civil war which tuck the content in an ocean of blood.

My president seemed to be an over ambitious man trying to bring Africa under the umbrella of the eastern awning. He had a sturdy and strapping sort of fortitude that blacks should be free and one, regardless of his/her national of racial background. That is why he supported and trained freedom combatants found at any bend of the continent.

"Hi gentleman, are you geared up to meet the terms of my contentment?" looking right into my petite eyes, he released his supervisory tongue like a sudden fall of rain. "Yes Sir." I replied gazing at his glittering murky black façade without even knowing what the operation is all about. In fact I had to respond that way, not the mode I know what will be waiting if I retort him otherwise. There is no prank and crack in wake. He is all the time straight forward. What he says is what he means, that is all. He, with his overriding tone of voice, screeched once again straight in to my diminutive ears, "I am optimist that you will execute it to the best of my pleasure and the pleasure of the entire Africa" and glanced at me from the tip of my hair down to the soul of my feet.

"Undoubtedly Sir!" I replied in to time, without taking a breathing space to gulp down the air I gasped. He doesn't want to hear words of trounce, 'We should not hesitate to bestow Devil his due" is his slogan. For him perplexity is the mother of collapse.

"I don't want to see Gahigy breathing any more in this shanty but succulent world. We as African leaders can't afford to tolerate him exterminate more people than what he has already slaughtered. We don't have to turn blind eyes to the tormented and distressed people of Kigali." and looked at his escorts. He doesn't have that brawny confidence on any roughly around him. He at times denies him own silhouette to be his hold under the beam of the sun.

His watchdogs have fully fixed their eyes on me. I was sure that they had an extraordinary control of my budge. Their temper and humor changes with the tenor of the president. When he feels hot, his blood moves like a cobra trying to cudgel and instantly their vessels will begin to puff out.

"Give him the letter!" the president roared. It took one of the watchdogs no time to bring and hand over it to me. I instantly scanned the substance in the letter and accepted the instruction in pleasure. What else could I do?

"You can process your trip right away and report your progress to me on this phone at every junction." He gave me six figures. "Gaily is a dangerous man, Tarkio. It needs meticulous finish up. That is why we chose you from our best intelligence T-4B Commando Brigades. Peerless wishes and forget not the reward at the successful completion of your mission in Rwanda!" In the early hours of the daylight of the morrow I had in Rwanda.

I told everything to my one day old spouse. She could not believe my departure on the morrow of my weeding." I cannot accept that as realistic, is this why he called you in few seconds time after the church ceremony of your marriage? Her question was followed by tender and scorching tears. "Yes, my striking lady. "I replied with a broken heart. I could not keep my tears bubbling like a water fall from the tip of my empathy. She continued sobbing following my snuffle.

For some times the situation in our tapered but comfy bed room was entirely changed. "How could you let me know such an awful news before my blood of virginity is dried?" she sustained in her nonstop bawling and howling." Is that the reward you have for me this night? Is it what I deserve from you? Questions after questions rained out of her mouth.

"What Can I do Say, what can I do? I am a army force. I cannot move an inch away from the command of my superiors, whether good or otherwise the word may be Mind you the instruction is from His Excellency president Menterashaw. You know how pig-headed and mulish-mended he is. If I rebuff his wave of order, you may loss me forever I am sure he will not hesitate to finish me before my friends like he did on others.

"I stated scroll of words to convince her but I could not get her out of her agony and stop her tears I could not help her except for speaking to the nucleus of her heart through my warm chops. As I was Kissing her, my within spontaneously drilled me "kiss her well, you may not get this maws any more! I did but could not be satisfied but what to do I do I had to make myself ready fore the trip. I am already booked for tomorrow morning flight early at 6:00 A.M.

Immersed in her tears, "By the way when will you be back?" she asked me as I was going out leaving her on that dwarf bed. "As soon as I fulfilled my mission, my darling" I tried to flash my façade tooth to hide my lamenting heart inside, "What is your mission?" She erected a question that I can not answer.

"I better tell you that when I return." I tried to chuckle even if it looked an expression of grief. "Please leave me alone and let me go, it is now quarter is to six. I hope we will meet again.

I left the room taking my ever ready bag from the panel. "Give me the last kiss, please" Her voice halted me from my way ahead and I got returned back to her .I kissed her, she kissed me, we kissed each other ... our lips, our emotion, our passion, everything cried with us. "I want you to let me go with pleaser?" I asked her. She gave me no response except for embracing me like a small kid in the middle of the breast of his mother.

It was the calks of the car that drove me to the airport that took me out of her caring and adoring arms. "Do not tell my going to anyone. "She did not act in response to my question, instead asked me where me where I am going. "I was not happy to tell her my mission land. "I will call you and tell soon." I kissed her once aging and left the room with out the knowledge of any other third person.

I was looking all around me as if I was seeking for assistance. Right away the woman who sat at my side in the flight asked me, "Can I help you as if trying to persist the chat we had while we were in the airbus." Well I don't stand like staying in a hotel. "She, without delay, took the words from my mouth and said "so what man ...? She shouted in laughter.

"I can take you home. You can stay with my family for some time. I hope you will feel at home there. My parents like Ethiopians. I was quit calm for sometimes. "Please don't hesitate to be with us." We looked each other for a fraction of minutes. "Are you Rwandan?" she nodded her head. "Tutus of…? She did not want me to call the other tribe by name. "I don want you to talk about them. The have finished us like lambs for slaughter "Really, did they kill so many people?"

"Yes, they did but I do not want to remember that savagery incident forget to talk about it. By the way, why are you coming to my land, sorry our land? Your people and we are …, I think we have same color but you are … oh you are the splendor look s of the continent. I love you very much." I could sense the vapor of love gushing out through the water of her eyes. "It was just three tender kisses that we had in the arduous flight. How on earth could she be the woman working for the same mission behind me without my knowledge?"

After a long vacillation "I accepted her invitation and went to her home to get rid of Saby's palely thought. I should not live yesterdays'. I must be able to live now and this moment. My existence must be a moment by moment reality. "Tomorrow is not mine; at least I am not sure whether to successfully perform my mission without being sacrificed. So I should let myself act at this instants like a dog." I simply told to my heart.

The city was a little hot. The crowned head of tranquility assumes ruling over the ins and outs of capital. It appears the hard rule has dictated the entire city not to breathe anything even a word. The whole complex is quite hushed. The living trees lined across the heart of the highway in the suburb take after the pillars of counterfeit greens. Nobody hikes around the comely street except for me, Marry and the driver.

I spent the hideous night of June 8 and went directly to my mission spot for scrutinize and if possible execute the order. I was quite an internationally recognized state squad. I was responsible for different assignations abroad. But now I am the secret agent of my beloved nation to defend national esteem and external relations. I knew what lies ahead when I started my operation. Though I was armed to the nose, there is still hesitation in my heart in the validity and certainty of the espionage conducted. I felt like calling Saby before I plunged in to this nasty work of avoiding Gahigy.

"Hello, is this Tariku, is speaking..." It seems she cloud not listen to my voice. Tears have taken her attention totally. "Where are you calling from?" she repeatedly asked me same question "Love you Saby." was she only answer I gave her. "I, too. Where did you spend the night? How is it going? When will you be back ..." so many questions, once again. My answer is never changed. I handed down after saying "I love you and soon I will be with you."

But my words could not impede her tears from plummeting like stream of water, feel. Indeed, the spirit of her heart was never a way from me even when I was with Mary the whole of the night. I could see faint dying light gleaming out of the window of palace. The paramount chief of Hutu the drama would end when I stabbed my sword in to the center of heart of Gahigy.

After a two weeks stay some how I managed to get in to the place and take a hiding place at one corner corrupting one of the security men therein with 1000.00USD. In fact when I told him my purpose he was pleased to welcome me without the spice I added to his pocket. It seems everybody does not like Gahigy. We chose you from our best intelligence T-4B Commando Brigades. Good luck!" the commanders last sentences slicked in my mind.

Then three minutes were left. I loaded my pistol and put my index finger across the trigger. I had obligation and responsibility granted from the then President of my nation. If I could wind up the mission successfully I would be rewarded one hundred thousand birr and be called a national hero.

Gahigy's house is fenced by land mines and there are gang ways that lead to the house. I saw the paths carefully on the map I had at hand and stealthily tip toed in to the darkness to Gahigy. I was also sure that the guards were dead asleep by then except for my assistant standing in dark which was about twenty meters away from Gahigy's bedroom.

When a loudspeaker suddenly boomed "Hands up! You are under arrest!" It was that same voice I had have the chance to here for the last 13 days. I had no time to hesitate my captivity than a butt of a machinegun knocked me off on my temple. Unconsciously I fell on the ground bleeding from the nose. I knew noting about what has happened later. But one thing stood crystal clear in my mind, I was nipped at the blooming into a respected national here of Ethiopia.

Sudden splash of water waked me up from my sleep when I opened my eyes; it was my mother standing before my bed.

Good heaven! I am not a prisoner! Sad I half unconscious prisoner! What are you talking about? You sleepy! Put on your clothes in the least possible delay. School is late otherwise; my mother reassured my being an ordinary student.

FANATICAL CHILD

Tesema Gutema is an outspoken sort of person. He is just expressive and extrovert. There was sensation and emotion in his words. Many could feel the spirit of bluntness in them. One could sense the insight of wisdom in him. He looks very cute, well dressed and charming. However, it is not that difficult to observe the agony babbling out from within deep in his heart. Pain and pang is vibrantly a part of his appearance. They are almost his everyday friends.

He mourns and yet he is grateful to God and says, "I have a good morning in the future, not a good mourning." I wanted to explore more about him.

Tesema lives alone. He hardly is 12 years old. "My family is a child headed family. There is only one person in the family and that is me. I have lost both my parents in two consecutive years, thanks be to AIDS. My father dead first four years ago and in a year time my mother followed him leavening me and my sister all alone for good." It seems as if he is mocking but he was serious about it. He never wants to demonstrate his sting and twinge outwardly.

It looks he has done too much of that kind. He has cried enough. Every morning he used to think of his parents most importantly his father and blubber holding his photo. "Crying …" He said "… can't bring change. It cannot get the lost ones back into the place. I was about to go mad as I was crying almost on everyday basis and quit school." He paused for a while and looked back the ups and downs that he has gone through in those short days of his life.

In some way, he continued to his demonstrative words. "However, thanks to my government they have thought me to stand on my own. It doesn't mind for its people. Humanity is never honored in its sight. I am comforted. I do not want to go back to the situation I was in years ago. Had it not been for their follow up and counsel, I would have been a crazy on the street. But God has rescued me from being such a fanatical kid, who has no one after him to give care." It looks he wishes to forget all about the past and stretch forward.

However, his only friend Chery was wondered as to how he handles life without parents at home. Chery lives on the street since the very date he lost all his parents. He used to always say: "Pleasure is a passage, not a goal. How can one have life without parents?" He always tries to pull him out of home. "How do you manage life? Where do you get you income to sustain the family?" Chery asked.

Tesema did not take time to address this question. "Well the God inside me supports us to the best of what is possible according the program that I am created for. As you well know I was awfully despaired when my father died. It was not without a reason. I was very much intimate with my father. He was like a friend to me. He used to give me love and care. I used to be well warmed by his arms, well cherished and treasured by him. You know ..."

He took some time for thinking and pondering. Tesema presume, and continued to say, "I had never thought of death before him. Believe me, I had no notion about it, what so ever. I never believed myself that my father is corporeal person. Nevertheless, I saw him dying; my whole being dead with him. You know, I used to depend on him and only him. He was like my God. In fact, his death has brought courage in. I am okay, I don't intend to get out of home and start life on the street."

Chery felt as if he just failed to remember to answer to his question, and gave him a kind of reminder on what has been left unanswered, "how do you manage life at home without parents? Do you get enough money to sustain you life. You see if you sell everything you have and join us for street life, the street itself will give you enough to eat, enough to eat, enough to company with ... what not? Is the home life good enough without parents?"

"It is not!"

"Hence, how do you sustain life at home?"

"Well, on my spare time I go for small works to support myself."

"Why you can always beg with us and get money three folds as the amount you get from your small business."

"I can't be beggary?"

"Why, I am not created to be so. None of us are created for that end. I wonder why we always depend on begging as an individual, as a group of people, as a society, as a nation?... we have to change our mind. We need to look into the home and try find out a solution from within. You see I have no one around and yet I don't want to look outside. I must dig out inside first, it is only then I may cry for a help. "

Cherry wasn't convinced.

"Yes Chery, what matters is not what comes from outside. The thing from within has a lot of power."

THE MOTHERLESS

Debre Zeit is one of the most beautiful quick-witted cities in the country. It is so striking that many would like to have their prized times there for leisure in it. It has countless eye-catching scenarios escorted by four crater and one synthetic lagoons with modestly temperate warmth. It is in deed a moving and gleaming city.

People run hear and there with full of joy, children play, the wind blow, the rivers run. Everything is in its dynamism, except for the five carter lakes in the town. Near one of the lakes, there is a small house made from mud. It is very narrow like a small pigeon hall. It has only one gate and window for ventilation, exist and entrance. Hewan and her sister hardly live in it.

As soon as I entered the house together with my friend Kebede Kassa, we meet Hewan and her sister around a small table eating their lunch. We greeted them. They welcomed us warmly. As the food on the table was so small, they could not dare to invite us to join them on the table. We waited until they are done with their lunch. Now we explained them the reason that has brought us there to their house to visit them. "I know." Helen replied and continued introducing herself to my readers and myself.

Here we go, "I am called Hewan. I am finishing my 20ᵗʰ years of age. I was born into a family of three children. All of us are females except for two boys who died at birth. I am the middle child in the family. My elder sister is now catching her 25. She was very good at her education, but thanks to poverty, she could not continue as she wished. Now she is a drop out. Yet she is thankful to the lord that she is married to a soldier and has one child. My younger sister is a blind woman. She, somehow, developed sight problem while she was a two-month-old child. However, my parents were not able to take her for medication, again due to poverty. Bit by bit, my sister got to be sightless. Now she is completely unsighted.

She is also thankful to the lord, that he has given her an opportunity to join the blind school at Addis Ababa. Now, she is about 18. She loves to be alone. I guess she has something deep in her mind that she never wants to share with the rest of us, something, going on between her and God."

Hewan is such a fast woman. Her words move quicker than a moving wind, and yet they are well constructed and to the point. She is a born bright sort of person. Her mind thinks deep but on the double. She is also a cleaver student in her school. She has won a necklace as an award by ranking first in her class for five consecutive years.

I asked her to tell me a little about her parents. She took a long breath and opened he mouth to narrate the story. "Well, to start with my father, I don't know him at all. I do not even have the slightest of his memory in my mind. In fact, my mother used to tell me that he passed away while I was a very little kid, a kid without tooth and memory. What I know was my mother. She was actually my mammy, my sister, my friend and what not? She was the only person I had in this planet earth. She is the one that has shared with me a love of parents. She has brought me up."

"Where and how is your mammy today?" I asked her very humbly. She looked at Kebede "Doesn't he know?" she asked him with her body language. He nodded "Yes" without words. From their gesturing, I came to know all about her mother. She is dead. Nevertheless, I wanted to listen it from her. Hewan has understood that I am waiting for her retort. She said, "She is dead" with words of hope and confusion, together. I continued to ask 'How and when?" Now Hewan came in to answer to those two questions of mine.

"Her death happened three years ago." She went explaining me the story.

"She was an HIV positive woman and as a result had been unwell for quite a long time." She panicked somehow and said "You see, I don't want to recall that moment of my life. Sorry, I cannot stand narrating the death of the only person I have in life. It was just on my arms that she left this world for good. No one was around, no body at all." She paused herself and after a while she continued with a kind of question.

"How can I be able to tell you such a story that etched in my mind now and then? It is unforgettable and yet I do not want to remember that panorama of the greatest tragic moment in my life at all. If I do, it makes me crazy, man!" She just exploded into tears."

I realized that I have to stop asking about her mother any more. Kebedew re-comforted her and after a little counseling we got her back into the dialogue.

MANAGING POVERTY

Debre Brihan is cold as usually. It was raining. Apart from the rainfall it was so chilly that one can't stand it without winter close and additional warm in the house. The road was grubby. Everybody has closed inside home with their traditional stove full of burring charcoal.

Elias and his brother Bedilu were going to Hana to discuss about the false marriage between Elias and herself, who have won the DV lottery recently. Hana is actually married to Abonesh and has one child called Gideon. She is despaired, very poor and leading life under destitution. The rain started while they were already half way to Hana's house.

They had no place to shelter themselves from the rain. The only option they had was to continue running to the house. Elias was thinking in mind that when they reach there they would have the habitual stove on and have some heat inside the house. Somehow after a 20 minutes walk they reached.

Elias said "This is their house." He frizzed in panic. I just couldn't believe my eyes. He saw up on the firmament. The cloud is riding over the blue. The downpour is still showery. The wind is moving swiftly. Now he looked down at the house. It is made of plastics. Both the wall and the roof are made up of plastic bags embroidered together to a very big size. The door, the windowpane, everything is made from a dozen of plastic bags. He just couldn't believe it.

Inside, Gideon, a 9 months old child, and his parents are living. He is the first borne to them. Three of them were sleeping all together on a kind mattress arranged on the ground, keeping the child in the middle, to warm him with their breath and body temperature. Their blanket is too old and too taut. There is no bedclothes to keep them warm. They embarrass each other to keep one another balmy; this how they lived over the gone three solid years of their matrimonial life.

As they entered the house, the mother came out of bed and welcomed them to her residence. Soon her husband came out of bed. He is in his normal close. It looks he doesn't have a nightdress to go to bed with. They wanted to let the guests sit down, but they have no such stuff in the house. There is no light in, no any electricity at all. What's more, there is no water, no latrine, and no kitchen, nothing at all. Elias couldn't believe his eyes. He just couldn't stand his emotion, the bubbling volcano deep within him.

"Is she the one that I am gonna singe marriage with?" His brother nodded yes. Elias doesn't look happy. Abonesh pulled him out and said "why do you care about the woman. It is a false marriage. You only want to get the chance to America that is all."

On the other hand, Kibrom is asking his wife "Is he the one who s going to buy my wife?"

"It is not selling myself. It is selling opportunity."

"How could you forget to write my name in the application form?"

"I have told you a number of times. It wasn't me who filled the form. It was my sister."

"Why didn't she put my name in the form?"

"That is gone." She shouted. "I don't want you to ask me questions that I can't answer. If you are happy, let's sell the opportunity. Have some money. I will go with him to the US and in three years time I will come back to collect my child and you. If you are not happy with this let's stop it here and continue our life as usual."

In the mean time Aboneh got back to home and asked "Can we discuss outdoor please. Now the rain has gone."

"Sure" Kibrom replied.

"We all are poor, even destitute. We lead a hand to mouth sort of life. We eat mostly ones or two times a day. There are also days we spend without food. All told, our everyday food is bread. Hence, we never get nutrient food at all. That is I guess the reason why we all want to go to America, leaving a lot things behind us." Abonesh started the discussion.

"Yes you are right. Leaving ones family behind is not an easy thing indeed." She plunged into tears. Her husband tried to encourage her to stop crying and continue with the discussion.

"Well, how much are we going to pay for the opportunity?" Abonesh asked.

Elias came in and said "Before that I would like to hear the concent of Kibrom."

"Well on my part it is Okay. She will singe for you and will take you to America as her husband as long as you can pay us the 50,000.00Birr in two phases."

"What a man?" Elias said deep in his inside. He just couldn't believe his words. "Have you discussed well the fact that it will take her quite a long time to take you and perhaps her child? You see, now after signing marriage with her will go to America and after a while will process for me. After taking me there she will process divorce and will thing of processing for you. This I am sure will take her over five years."

"I know. I can see the hard time. But we are trying to mange poverty." Kibrom replied.

"Well in that regard, I will give her 10,000.00 Birr when she singes for me and another 10,000.00 Birr when she leaves to America. In fact I will also cover all the cost it takes her to America."

Kinrom came in and asked, First of all the payment is for me not her."

"That I don't mind. If you two agree Ii will do it the way you want it to happen."

"Good, how about the rest of the money?"

"Well the rest of the money I will give you when I am about to leave to America."

Abonesh and Hana are out of the game. The thing is between Kibrom and Elias. "Well you must pay 60% in the first two phases. The remaining 40% when your case is done and when you are about to leave to the US. Is that Okay with you?"

Finally, they agreed and fixed time for the first action. Hana is halfhearted but Kibrom is, however, ready to sell his marriage and eager to collect the money.

A PRICELESS GIFT

"It would rather be easier for me to tell you what my mother hasn't done for me than narrating what she has, which for me is like trying an ocean by a small spoon." It was this way that Lidia started telling me all about the success stories that she has achieved. She is indeed a woman of vigor with a fain-looking appearance. One can clearly see the sprit of good jollity and exuberance moving all across the border of her chocolate colored face.

"Do you know the fact that I have no any other close relative than my grandmother?" She forwarded a question to me. I kept mum, putting my hands on my mouth. "Yes, I lost my mother while I was still a child. She was a bed ridden woman, almost unable to go for a doctor due to paucity of enough resources at hand, most importantly due to lack of enough riches for medical pay." She quitted her narration for a while, breathing deep into her inside as if she is trying to inhale her tears and emotion, all together.

After a while she continued, "She died in 1994, by then I was a grade 3 student, just a little kid. That same year, my father who also followed the footsteps of his wife to the church land in four years time was also under par to the bed. Had it not been for my grand mama, I would have stopped from going to school that year and become somebody else today."

Again, she took a break and came out of the melancholy that has buried her totally in the pat, "You just can imagine what life would look like for three children who don't know their left and right properly when they loose their parents within a gap of four years time? We just became a child headed family. Everything fall on the shoulder of my elder brother who himself was a student by then, I tell you, we felt as if the whole world quieted for three of us together with our parents. We became hopeless, as no one was around to take care of us and look after us. It was in this critical moment of my life that grand mama was born to my family as a new parent. She is a priceless gift, a gift from God above."

Her grand mama was living in the US. She went while my mother was some months old. Since then they have never met. It is after a along time that she came back home.

"The gone is gone, thank God I don't want to lift it up again and be worried about it. You know what I am saying. I do not want to cry over the spattered milk. I want to remember just the good things that the good God has done for me over the years. It was almost form the tummy of a lion that my grand mama rescued my life and that of my brothers. Now I am not as I was before. I have a future."

I interrupted her and asked, "How do you come to recognize Jesus in your life?" My grand mama used to teach us every day about Him and only Him. The way she teach you about this profound Person and God really makes you love Him and from the heart. He is the King of kings in my life, the Lord of lords, what not? " She almost got into tears again. Her affection for Jesus is now babbling out in the form of hidden teardrops.

However, I just could not give her much time to pour out her emotion that way and took her to my next question. "What impression do you have from your grand mama?" It really did not take her time to respond to the question very swiftly.

"Well what impress me most is that I have more a mother, a father... I have everything I need for life. She is a good friend and a good teacher... what not? America has thought her how to be good for others. Together with us she has about 15 children. Twelve of us, she took them from the street. They have no parents as well. They has no body to give them due care. The government didn't do anything good for them. They were hopeless like us. Nevertheless, this woman has brought them a hope from abroad while so many of us in the country couldn't even think well about them. Shouldn't we reach our hands to reach the poor around us?"

She raised a difficult question to react in practical terms. She came again and continued to say "Somehow, we have become to be a society that receives. When do we start giving man?

Unexpectedly she plunged into tears. She shouted and sobbed for a while. I just couldn't understand the motive behind her tears. I tried to stop her but couldn't manage to get her back into a better situation. I finally decided to leave her alone till she gets back in to the mood.

Right away she was okay. Now she has started cleaning her tears from her face. I asked why she got into tears all of a sudden. "I am afraid; we will remain poor up until we start giving from the little we have. Isn't it so? Isn't that the secret of those blessed countries all over the world? I am wrong my brother? … " She replied to my question with a dozen of other questions.

THE YOUNG PROFESSOR

Dr. Solomon Asefa is quite a young man having a promising futurity in his life. He looks quite energetic, passionate and playful. Solomon works for the Addis Ababa University in the department of foreign language and literature. He has been teaching in some other university before joining this one two years back as a student working for his second PhD in Linguistics and as a teaching staff in the aforesaid department. .

By the time I went to his office, he was so busy, may be as busy as bees, with many students surrounding his desk for diverse services. Some are born-again Christians, some have political intersect, and some are for academic purpose. But he has time for all of them and in fact sends them all in great satisfaction. He has a lot of smiles and good words for them. Many of his friends say that "Solomon knows the langue of students." Actually he does. He speaks to their heart.

They love him. They want to stay with him. For most of them he is a role model. Many would like to take after him. I stayed outside of his office until he finishes with the students who are his advices. Latter, he gave me his kind "Come in" invitation and I did accordingly.

As soon as I am in his office, he shut the door behind me, curtained the winds and let me sit down. I was not strange with what has been doing. He usually do the same whenever I am in his office, in fact, for good reason. "Why did you come before the fixed time?" I saw my watch. I am a little before our time.
"Sorry"
"No you must take care. The days are going worsened. There are hundred one eyes behind us. You know what has happened yesterday?"
"No, I have no idea."
I was eager to listen to him. Dr. Solomon Asefa is among the very few but very well respected university scholars. He looks quite young but very well educated. He more than two masters degrees apart from his PhD and two other first degrees. So far, he has published three teaching materials, two novels and two collections of short stories and poems. He is in fact a very well read and versed man that knows and does literature.

"Well, yesterday two people came to my office."
"What type of people and at what time?" I like questioning.
"Well I just can't tell?"
"Who do you think that they could be?"

His mobile rang. "Sorry, it is Pastor." he said continued to talk to him. Dr. Solomn believes in God. He is a borne-again Christian. He preaches and teaches in his church of Jesus Christ. He is a well renowned inexhaustible person among the evangelical Christians. He has pioneered more than one church here and there.

"Well, he wants me to preach next Sunday to his congregation." He summarized his conversation.

"That is wonderful!"

"Why wonderful?"

"I like when people like you preach the gospel?

"Why?"

"I don't know, but I always feel that the gospel would get power when it is from you people."

"Do not go astray. Gospel is not by education, it is by the power and mighty of the Holy Spirit, period!"

I didn't want to argue. He is such a well read person that he has all the reasons to convince me easily. No one can stand long arguing with him. That is how it goes. I just wanted him to get back to the reason why both us are here today. But, I want him to let me know those people who came yesterday to his office.

"Can I get you back to our discussion? Who think those people were?"

"I guess they are agents of this government. You know they misunderstand me a lot. I guess they are not happy with my relationship with you."

"Why?"

"I am sure somehow they have come to know that there is no any love relationship between us. You know what one of them have said 'you better stop your evils with Suzan. We have come to know that she is never your girlfriend. You two have a specials mission.' I asked him "what mission he is talking about and he replied "political' in short and the other one coming in between us 'Take care. We came to advise you to take care only.' For your surprise they have told me the name of my wife and children."

I was a bite worried. "How could they come to think that way?" I asked myself but I just couldn't get a kind of enjoyable answer to my own question. We have many to talk about our love relationship. We go everywhere together, including in the church, so that the university community and all other people around us may not think of our relation different.

I was eager to learn the end of the story and asked him "What then" Dr. Solomon took sometime and said "Then they left. They left the office."

"Does it mean we have to break for sometimes?" I asked him softly.

"Break what?"

"May be our being together?"

"That is dangerous. It would be like saying what you have thought of us is perfectly right."

"What measure should we taken then? Should we stop bringing new people to the Kingdome of Christ?"

"You see they have misunderstood us."

"How?"

"I guess, they feel we are recruiting students to opposition parties?"

"How?"

"That is what it is?"

Both of us kept quiet for some time. We were not sure what to do next. "It is amazing."

"What is amazing?" Dr. Solomon asked.

"I have never heard of any government in history that never respects its own constitutions, laws, and regulations. Freedom of belief, for instance is clearly stated in the constitution and yet they don't want you to preach the gospel and snatch souls for the hands of the strongholds." I was speaking from the heart. Dr. Solomon tried to mock.

"Well the best thing is to pray for a week or so and see what wisdom God will give us to run His purpose in our life. Otherwise, these people are already made mad with the public. They can do anything they wish."

"I know what you mean. You remember why they put Dr. Mathiwosto jail; it is because they misunderstood him. Somehow they confused him as member of the party of coalition for unity and democracy."

"Well they have taken all the due steps before putting him to jail."

"What?" I was surprised.

"For instance, they have warned him not to be popular among the students." He mocked again. He highly depends on his Lord. He takes things simple and leave them to the will of the Lord.

"I think they have killed him in the prison."

"Are you serious?"

"Even if I am not, they can do it? They don't mind. They didn't even mind to dismiss over 40 most respected and adored university professors only because of their difference in their political opinion."

All of a sudden the door was knocked. Both of us were worried. But Dr. Solomon opened it after a while. It was those people who came again. Four of us stood on our feet and saw each other. Right away, one of them showed his identity card for both of us and said "Okay, now you are under arrest."

I said "For what, for preaching the Gospel?"

"Well that is not what we can discuss here. Now we want you to go direct to the nearby police station. Period!" He put his ID back.

All of a sudden we left the office under their custody.